John Hervey Ashworth

Rathlynn

Vol. 1

SALZWASSER
VERLAG

John Hervey Ashworth

Rathlynn

Vol. 1

Reprint of the original, first published in 1864.

1st Edition 2022 | ISBN: 978-3-75259-459-1

Verlag (Publisher): Salzwasser Verlag GmbH, Zeilweg 44, 60439 Frankfurt, Deutschland
Vertretungsberechtigt (Authorized to represent): E. Roepke, Zeilweg 44, 60439 Frankfurt, Deutschland
Druck (Print): Books on Demand GmbH, In de Tarpen 42, 22848 Norderstedt, Deutschland

RATHLYNN.

RATHLYNN.

BY

THE AUTHOR OF

"THE SAXON IN IRELAND."

"Oh, how full of briars is this work-a-day world!"
As You Like It.

IN THREE VOLUMES.

VOL. I.

LONDON

1864.

RATHLYNN.

CHAPTER I.

> "All places that the eye of Heaven visits
> Are, to a wise man, ports and happy havens."
>
> *King Richard II.*

It was the close of the year 1848 when I stepped on board the "Llewellyn" steam-packet, at Kingstown, and bade, in all probability a long, if not a last, adieu to Ireland. We had a rough passage, and the majority of those on board suffered severely. But when we once more trod the land all past inconvenience seemed to be forgotten. At one o'clock in the morning we sat down to a plentiful supper in the admirable refreshment rooms at the Holyhead station. Much did I marvel to observe how soon the Saxon stomach can recover its vigour; and, with astonishment, I saw men, who not an hour ago had been prostrate and helpless, become suddenly lively and brisk, partaking with hearty good-will of lamb and salad, chicken and ham, and washing down the same with long draughts of bitter beer!

It is at best a comfortless journey from Galway to London, embracing little worthy of notice to while away the tedious hours. And the packets, moreover, are at present too small, so that there is a mighty rush for berths, and sad is his lot who is compelled to make his couch on a few ricketty chairs, or on the hard, inodorous floor of the cabin.

It was late in the afternoon that I reached the house of my relative, Mr. Rosse. He was the only brother of my father's first wife; but so intimate had been the relation ever kept up between them, that, from my earliest years, I had been accustomed, not only to call, but to consider him as my uncle. He was a man of literary tastes and simple habits, went little into the world, but loved to scan it from his "loophole of retreat." His farm, his woods, his fishery, and his game were his out-door objects of interest, and—except that, as a magistrate, he attended sessions and county meetings—he was rarely seen beyond the precincts of his own domain. Though verging on seventy years, and an occasional martyr to gout, the hereditary disease of his family, he was still a hale and vigorous old man, retaining in his form and features manifest indications of a tranquil and temperate life.

He was a bachelor, and kept up an establishment more for comfort than for show. An old butler and housekeeper, with a few inferior domestics, a groom and gardener who had cottages close by, sufficed him, for he studiously avoided the usual visitings of the neighbourhood. His relatives, however, and the friends of his earlier years always met with a kind welcome, and all agreed in declaring that "Penrhôs" was the pleasantest house in the whole county.

It was evening, when, having travelled three long stages from Bangor, traversing some of loveliest scenery in Wales, I found myself at the small town in the vicinity of which my relative resided. As the walk was not three miles, and the weather delightful, I left my luggage to be forwarded, and proceeded on foot. Following the path through green meadows, along the margin of a rushing river, I soon reached the entrance gates leading to Penrhôs. It was massive, substantial, and simple, and though there were neither sham turrets nor sham portcullises, nor a damp, gloomy rustic gothic lodge, nor huge iron gates bedizened with blue and gold, still the whole was managed with such good taste that the passer-by would pause to observe it, and pass on with a gleam of satisfaction.

Entering the gate, the road wound gently upwards, in some places cut through the solid rock, while here and there a primeval oak threw far and wide its gnarled and mossy branches, forming overhead a lofty arch of the most refreshing verdure. As the ascent proceeded the woods became more dense, but frequent breaks in the foliage allowed the sunbeams to penetrate, though no view was yet to be gained of the open country below. Nor, indeed, on approaching the house could any idea be formed of the singular beauty of the situation, for, standing before the ancient porch, the eye roamed up the mountainous heights above, embracing merely the higher portion of the domain. But this was wild and striking. Two lofty peaks, east and west, were penetrated and divided by a deep glen, down which roared a never-failing torrent of the purest water; while alders, and stunted oaks, and numerous old and fantastic thorns, intermingled with the silver birch, fringed the margin of the stream, and straggled in picturesque clumps almost to the very summits of the mountains. Among these rocky heights might flocks of sheep be seen, cropping the scant but delicious herbage; while below, on a level with the house, where the lands were more alluvial and fertile, horned cattle of the most approved breeds were quietly grazing, or patiently ruminating, beneath the grateful shade.

Nevertheless, Mr. Rosse was no improver, in the modern acceptation of the term—the place was, in its general features, such as he had inherited it from a long line of ancestors; the first of whom, a Norman baron, one Gilbert de Rhos, had married Angharad, the only daughter and heiress of Madoc-ap-Griffydd-ap-Bleddyn, of Drwys, afterwards changed to Penrhôs, in one of the maritime counties of North Wales. There was a rude portrait in the great hall, supposed to represent this lady. She was tall, and of a stern-looking physiognomy, wore a high-crowned hat, with a gold band and buckle, and an immense frill surmounting a long dark cloak, which almost reached the ground.

The mansion, though of ancient and rude masonry, was interesting as a good example of the abodes of the Celtic magnates of former days. It had its massive square tower of three stories, the parapet divided on each side by one narrow embrasure. The arrow-slits below, and the lancet windows above, were still preserved. In fact, the whole building—with its many irregular gables, its deep mullioned windows, its grotesque corbels, and lofty dormer windows—gave the idea of being the work of several generations.

The interior was in strict keeping with the exterior—much panelling of dark oak, ceilings loaded with huge cornices and rude devices, a spacious hall, with its dais and music-gallery, and, to crown all, a staircase formed of solid blocks of oak, with grotesque newells and massive banisters. Yet an air of perfect cleanliness and comfort pervaded the whole, and though sundry tables, and chairs, and wardrobes, and chests were very ancient, black as ebony, and carved in rude and deep relief, yet the beds were of modern construction, and every recently discovered requisite of luxury and comfort was supplied with unsparing abundance.

It was in this interesting spot that I spent many of the happiest days of my boyhood. I could hunt, shoot, or fish *ad libitum.* My uncle Rosse was never so happy as when he promoted the happiness of everyone around him, and I was only too glad to escape for awhile from my paternal home, where my father, Admiral Wyville kept up a species of discipline which was much akin to that of the quarter-deck.

My reception at Penrhôs was as cordial as ever — my good uncle was pleased to say that I had gained much in manly appearance, and old Howell, the butler, gazed with admiration at the once spare and somewhat delicate boy whom he had loved to pamper and indulge.

"Cot pless me, Master Frank!" said he, rubbing his hands together as was his wont—"you will be a man, and a fine man, after all, I declare."

It was not till after some days had elapsed, that my uncle Rosse began to question me about my sojourn in Ireland, and he was so minute and particular in his inquiries, that at length I was induced to confess that I had written a history of what befell me there during that period, and even that I had some thoughts of publishing the results of my short experience of the country for the benefit of future settlers.

"Of course, then," said my uncle, "as

you have confessed to the guilt of authorship, or rather perhaps, as I ought to say, the folly, you will best answer my queries by reading to me what you have written. As we dine at five o'clock, I can give you an hour after dinner in my study for the purpose. Will that suit you?"

"Perfectly," answered I, "but I fear you will find but little to interest *you* in my narrative. To you Ireland is as a foreign soil."

"Not so," replied he, "I was stationed at Athlone when I attained my majority in the Buffs, and I can assure you, Frank, that I saw no little of the world before I buried myself in this hermitage. I always felt a great interest in Ireland, and shall be very glad to hear your opinion of the country and the people. We will commence this very evening."

The study, to which Mr. Rosse was wont

to retire after dinner, was like everything else at Penrhôs, curious and complete in its kind. The panels of the ceiling were ornamented with heraldic devices, coloured and partly gilded; the walls were covered with book-shelves, boldly and grotesquely carved, and no carpet concealed the handsome and highly polished parquetted floor, made of richly veined oak, and put together two centuries before by some native genius in the art of inlaying. The chimney-piece had been taken from an old and neighbouring abbey, at the time of the great church spoliation, and the very chair which my uncle Rosse occupied was said to have belonged to the last abbot.

It was into this room that we entered on the eve of that very day.

"I am ready for you now, Frank," said he, as, having filled his meerschaum, he seated himself in the aforesaid chair on the right of the fire-place. "I never thought," continued he, "to see one of the family an author, for your ancestors, and mine too, have ever been more partial to the sword than to the pen. Nor do you look the author—I should rather take you for a young officer of dragoons."

"My dear sir," replied I, eagerly, "I do not pretend to the character either of a student or a literary man, but, considering that I have spent some time in a foreign country, it is natural to expect that I should be able to give some account of it."

"Do you call Ireland a foreign country?"

"Indeed the majority of the English know as little about it as they do of Cochin China, though it lies at their own door. In my narrative I merely state a few of my own impressions, and give such a peep into the habits and manners of the people as a short but eventful residence enabled me to do."

"Well, Frank, whatever your book may purport to be—a history of the people—a description of the country—or a series of startling personal adventures—or a little of all these jumbled together—a book is a book, and as such I shall undertake to criticize and give my opinion as the narrative proceeds."

"Thank you, sir," replied I, "the remarks of a person of your discernment and extensive reading will be most useful and acceptable to one so new as myself to the arts of composition."

"Prettily said, Frank; one more remark and you shall commence. I love what is natural in conception, in expression, and in action. If I take up a work and it begins thus: 'The night was dark and stormy,' or 'The moon shed her pale and pensive beams on the ivy-clad tower of ——,' or, 'The Vesper bell was flinging its deep and solemn sound, &c., &c.,' I close it at once, for I conclude that the style and sentiment will probably be turgid and unnatural. I like a book, even if a fiction, to commence as if the writer was about to tell the truth, that is, that he will be true to nature. Mark the quiet, simple mode in which John Bunyan and Daniel Defoe introduced their subjects in two of the most popular fictions that ever issued from the press. And so Dr. Samuel Johnson, in his tour to the Hebrides, has given all future tourists a quiet, truthful, and sensible example of style and matter, which, if they write, they would do well to imitate."

"I fear, then," said I, "you will find much to condemn in my few pages. Dr. Johnson felt and wrote as a philosopher, not as an enthusiast, and I allow that his depth of thought and vigour of style left nothing to be desired. But it would be mere folly for me to aspire to such eagle flights in the fields of literature; I only profess to describe what I saw, and what I felt, and what happened to me, in the homely style of a mere agriculturist and settler in the country."

"Don't fret yourself on that score, my dear boy," said my uncle, laughing. "I do not expect to find a Samuel Johnson in Frank Wyville, I do assure you. I shall be quite satisfied if I do not find a Baron Munchausen; so go on. But stay," continued he, after a pause, "one more remark and I have done. If it is, after all, as I suspect, a novel that you have been writing; if, I say, your hero is a blacksmith, or a gamekeeper, or your heroine a Methodist preacher, close your manuscript, it is of no earthly use beginning to read it to me."

"But, sir," rejoined I, "these anomalies take with the public — they must have something out of the beaten path to surprise them into attention."

"It may be so, but I think these exaggerations are productive of mischief. I am not for fishing up high intellect, and a thousand interesting attributes from among the common herd, and making heroes and heroines of worthy mechanics or unsavoury fishwomen."

"But you forget, sir," replied I, "as I am my own hero, and am in no wise likely to fall in love with a gamekeeper's daughter, I can be in no way amenable to your just remarks. So far, at least, my pages may pass review."

"Then let us commence. You must pardon my interruptions as well-meant. If I sleep, Frank, don't wake me. You may proceed."

CHAPTER II.

MY NARRATIVE.

"Now safe returned, with wand'ring tired,
No more my early home I'll leave,
And many a tale of what I've seen,
Shall while away the winter's eve."
H. K. White.

I HAD now left college for two years, and my conduct there had met with my father's approval. I took a respectable degree, had high testimonials from my tutors, and, fortunately, had avoided any scrape that could in any degree impugn my character for steadiness and prudence. My debts were accordingly cheerfully discharged; they were not large, and I remained at home assisting the admiral in the management of his patrimonial estate, and enjoying myself, and gaining health, strength, and activity, in the ardent pursuit of field-sports. But this was not to last for ever, nor did I wish it. My great anxiety was to travel and visit foreign lands, but as at present my father seemed averse to it, I did not venture to press the subject, well knowing that such a course would only have the effect of postponing my wishes to an indefinite period.

One morning, as I was going out to shoot, my father proposed to walk with me.

"You said a few days ago, Frank, that you wished to commence life in earnest?"

"I did, sir, I feel I ought to do something."

"Then read this letter, and let me know what you think of it."

It was from one Mr. McDeed, an Irish attorney. A portion of my late mother's fortune, it appeared, had been a mortgage upon an estate in the north-west of Ireland, from the proprietor of which neither principal nor interest could ever as yet be recovered.

"The Encumbered Estates Court," continued Mr. McDeed, in his epistle, "will now set matters to rights at once. Send up your petition to the Court, with an accurate statement of accounts, and a speedy sale is inevitable, and, so far as the proceeds go, your claims will be satisfied. Let me, therefore, have your instructions, &c."

"What, sir, is the amount to be recovered?"

"Including common interest," replied my father, "five thousand three hundred pounds and over. A good round sum, which, if recovered, would pay for those meadows and the extensive sheep-walk, which you know I have so long wished to purchase, as they adjoin our lands."

"I presume, sir, you wish me to conduct the matter?"

"I do, Frank; and more than this. If the estate does not fetch in the court the sum I have named, purchase it for me; I am told it is valuable, and then go there yourself, and devote your energies to improve and develope it."

I hesitated.

"I know nothing of Ireland or the Irish —I fear, sir, you will find me but an incompetent agent."

"I shall not expect too much—do your best; the employment will be instructive, and even interesting. You may observe much, and profit by it."

It was, therefore, arranged that I was to go, notwithstanding the tears and remonstrances of my only sister, Eleanor, who insisted that I was sure to be shot, and who informed my father, as a fact she had been often assured of, "that an Irishman cared no more for murdering a Protestant than eating a potato."

I met Mr. McDeed in Dublin, and as the biddings for Rathlynn did not cover the debt, I became the last bidder, and the admiral the proprietor of an estate the exact locality of which he could not even have pointed out in the Ordnance map.

Having communicated the result, and written for further instructions, I received by return of post a lengthened reply, from which I extract a few passages:

"As you do not object to remain in Ireland for a season, to superintend affairs there, it must be on these conditions—that you never be cajoled into gambling of any kind—that you will not, under whatever provocation, be wicked and foolish enough to fight a duel—and that you do not marry an Irish girl. The English are generally much taken with the fair Hibernians, for they are often beautiful, oftener winning; but I have other views for you. If you go to reside at Rathlynn, I shall consider you bound in honour to observe these conditions."

I smiled as I read these words, and packing up my things, prepared to commence my journey on the following morning.

Everybody who has been in Ireland knows what a dull, uninteresting flat a great portion of the interior of the island is. At the time I write, for twenty or thirty miles westward of Dublin, you would almost think a hostile army had recently passed over it. There is an appearance of dreariness, neglect, and desolation which powerfully affects the traveller, and he wonders, as he passes rapidly along, how it is that lands so adapted for the richest culture should be either marred or left untouched by the hand of man. Before half my journey was concluded, I left the railroad, and proceeded westward, in one of those strange-looking four horse cars, which carry from ten to fourteen passengers, one half *dos-à-dos* to the other. I do not dislike these rude, jolting vehicles—there is a variety about them—you see one-half the country, as you go, admirably well, and as you return, you enjoy the other half as if travelling through a new region.

I found myself seated near an elderly "gent," whose demeanour and dress bespoke him a person who ought to be known. He had on a loose drab over-coat, with trowsers of the same, a blue silk under-vest, and a stock of the old military cut. At a distance he looked very respectable, and nodded familiarly to several well-dressed ladies, and addressed our Jehu in a condescending and easy style, but, on a closer view, his somewhat soiled linen, and the indifferent texture of his clothing, reduced him considerably in the social scale.

As soon as the horses started he started too, and question followed question so rapidly, that I had scarcely the opportunity, even if I had the inclination, to answer.

"Of course you are going west," inquired he. I nodded assent.

"By your appearance you are a foreigner."

"No, I am English."

"We here call everybody born out of the country a foreigner, be he French, German, English, or anything else. A tourist, I suppose," continued he, "come to spy out the nakedness of the land?"

"And of the people," I replied with a smile.

"An asy task that, anyhow," said he, laughing, "now, young gent, let me tell you that you are fortunate in meeting with me; I can give you every kind of information you may require—I know the four provinces as well, or better that any man in them, statistically, historically, genealogically, geographically, and geologically. In fact, sir, my name, you will doubtless know it at once, my name is Stamer. I cater for the public—I arrange monster trips by sea and land—I bring tourists together—teach them that union is economy, and that by masterly arrangement both time and money may be saved, and much more real enjoyment secured."

"You are indeed, then, a benefactor to your species," said I, willing to fall in with his humour.

"Yes, sir, I consider myself so, I assure you. And now let me ask you how you propose to proceed when our car reaches its destination at Letterkenny?"

"I shall walk; the country, I am told, is wild and pleasant."

"Walk! I thought so," said he, giving me a look of genuine pity. "The country wild and pleasant—by dad, and it's wild enough, let alone pleasant. Now, young sir, allow me to give you one word of advice. I object to any respectable tourist walking. It is not gentlemanly—do you ever meet one of the House of Lords walking? Experience will teach any rational being that to perambulate a country is more fatiguing and more expensive then riding."

"More expensive? reiterated I, "how can that be?"

"Plain enough. I will give you an example. You know Wales?"

"Well."

"It was only last summer I was arranging a tour to embrace Snowdonia and its wonders,—Cader Idris—Arran—the Arrenigs, &c. I met three pedestrians at Corwen, and argued the matter with them. One was convinced, and took his seat alongside me to Dolgelly, the other two would walk. They were all, I suspect, Liverpool clerks, though they assumed aristocratic manners.

"Well, sir, what was the issue? My companion from the top of the stage coach had a charming view of the country, and every passing object was pointed out and explained to him. An expenditure of ten shillings housed him in Dolgelly just as the rain began to pour down, and he was in time to secure a good supper and comfortable bed. Now mark the case of his obstinate companions. Ten long miles they trudged on to Bala, and there dined. Eighteen miles more to Dolgelly, but the rain overtook them soon after they started, and they returned to Bala, wet to the skin. There they slept. Next day it rained heavily till noon, when they again started, got among the mountains as far as Drws-Nant, when the clouds actually poured down a deluge; they took shelter in a smoky cabin by the roadside for two hours or more—no use, on they go again through the mud and mire, wet as if they had been over-head in a mill-pool, reach Dolgelly at half-past eleven at night, and find all the beds at both hotels occupied! Now, sir, draw the balance. The riding tourist spent ten shillings—saw everything, and got in warm and dry. The pedestrians arrived dead-beat—no beds to be had—lost a day—saw nothing—spoiled their clothes and their tempers, and all at a cost of at least one third more than their more judicious companion—so much for pedestrians. I never see a young fellow painfully toiling along a dusty or muddy road, with his knapsack on his back, thinking more of his dinner in prospect than the prospect before him, that I do not say to myself, ten years hence he'll know better, or he's a regular ommadawn!"

I was much amused with my companion, who, under all his eccentricities, had a substratum of good sense, and I got many useful hints from him relative to the country whither I was bound.

"Now, sir," said he, "your Englishman is a regular grumbler, and, when he takes it into his head, a terrible scolder. Only hear him if anything goes wrong! Now in this part of the creation it's of no earthly use. Grumbling and scolding get nothing. You may spare your breath. Whatever comes, a joke and a laugh is the only way for it. Pat does not like scolding, except maybe from the landlord or the agent. It offends his dignity, but give him the kind word and the merry look, and he's your slave."

In answer to my question as to what kind of a country I was going into,—

"You may well ask that," replied he, "it's the old possession of the Red Hugh or Roe O'Donnel, and many a hard knock you English got there before the Plantation scheme settled the matter. Egad then, it's a queer country entirely—it's the ugliest and prettiest country on the face of the earth. But here we are at Letterkenny, so fare ye well, young gent, and remember my advice—a car and a horse are better and cheaper any day in the year than shanks mare."

Leaving my luggage to be forwarded by the first opportunity, I started early next morning on foot, having a knapsack strapped over my shoulders, and a good staff of English oak in my hand. As I moved off, I looked up at the windows of the hotel, perchance I might catch a glimpse of my friend Mr. Stamer, but as he was not visible I had the pleasure of thinking that he was still under the impression that he had made a convert of me. The morning was fine, with a cold north wind, and, spite of my friend's argument of the preceding day, I felt it was more desirable to keep myself warm with walking than to sit shivering on the outside of a car.

For ten miles I found the country undulating and bare of trees, and the chill wind whistling in sudden blasts over the dreary and half-cultivated expanse, gave a character of desolation and wretchedness to the whole scene. Indeed nothing looks so cheerless as a half-cultivated district, treeless, half-enclosed — with ruined fences, scantily populated, and even more scantily stocked with cattle. The original denunciation, "Cursed is the ground for thy sake" rose to my mind, as nothing but misery, squalidness, and neglect extended around me as far as the eye could reach. As I gazed upon this uninteresting tract I marvelled that my countrymen envied the Red Hugh his wild territory and his wilder subjects, and I could not but think "the undertakers" of James's times were bold men to sit down here with man and nature equally their foes.

But as I sped onwards matters began to improve. The path I was following, it could scarcely be called a road, sunk from the extensive table-land I had been traversing into a broad valley, and after crossing this the country became rugged and mountainous, with deep glens and gorges, and here and there lovely lakes reposed in the bosom of the hills. Sometimes on the bleak ridge of a hill, or low down by the margin of a marshy bog, might be seen a few cabins clustering together, but they were mere eye-sores, and often spoiled a scene where nature had lavished her choicest gifts. Cabins! why, the wigwam of a red Indian is a palace to many of these—they shock the eye of a stranger—they look the personations of fever and ague—to describe them in all their filth and wretchedness is too painful to attempt. They are at once a disgrace to the landlord, to the priest, and to the occupier. To the landlord, that he cares so little for those from whom he derives his income; to the priest, that he does not preach up a crusade against them; to the occupier, that he for one moment endures them.

As I travelled on and on all still was wretchedness wherever man was congregated. I had never witnessed such neglect in my own country, and was not prepared for it even here, though I had read and heard enough on the subject to make these scenes not unfamiliar to my mind. The reality I had never dared to conceive.

As I sat down under shelter of a huge boulder of granite, and by a spring that bubbled up from beneath it, to enjoy the plain fare I had the precaution to bring with me, a feeling of despondency crept over me, and I half repented the task I had undertaken; and when I looked around me on the interminable wastes, the craggy, barren mountains, and the entire absence of any habitation which could be construed into that of a gentleman or even a comfortable farmer, I was tempted to smile at the Admiral's three injunctions, the breach of any of which seemed an utter impossibility.

It was evening, when, after crossing a lofty mountain range, I saw the waves of the Atlantic in the far distance, and below me a small town occupying a bold eminence on the banks of a tidal river. The scene was striking, and not dissimilar to many of the views I had seen of Italy, and the shores of the Adriatic. As I stood gazing on the prospect from the slope of the mountain I had just crossed, a man with bare legs and feet, and with no covering on his long matted hair, came by driving a few goats before him. I beckoned to him, and he at once came to my side, but shook his head with a good-humoured smile, as much as to say, "I don't speak English." As I pointed, however, to various objects, as the town and the river, he gave me their names, and when I mentioned Rathlynn and the name of the former proprietor, Mr. Ryan, he pointed to a range of wild broken-looking hills far to the south-west, and pointing with his finger downwards pronounced the word "Lough." I understood by this that the place of my destination was among those mountains, and probably on the banks of some inland lake.

It was nearly dark, when after passing

over a bridge of fourteen arches, and climbing a steep ascent crowned by an ancient church and the remains of a castle, I found myself housed in the only "hotel" in the place. There was a huge turf fire on the hearth, the glare from which threw a half comfortable aspect over an apartment very scantily furnished. "And this is an 'hotel,'" thought I, looking round me disconsolately "Well, I am in for it, and there is nothing now for me but patience and endurance, till I am once more back again in dear old England."

I soon discovered from the noise and bustle below that the "Desmond Arms Hotel" was also a general shop and whisky-store, and consequently crowded with a number of poor, wild-looking creatures, who were content to give a hundred per cent. profit for every little article they were in need of. I had ordered tea and a mutton-chop. I could wish any of my English readers to have seen the latter—chop it was not, but a burned, blackened piece of carrion, that would have made a dog hesitate ere he touched it. The bread, however, was tolerable, and the tea not to complain of. Tired with my long walk, I ventured to stretch my limbs on a sofa, having a dirty cover over it, "all tattered and torn." In a moment I was sprawling on the floor—the head and two legs gave way. It was meant, evidently, as many things are in Ireland, for show and not for use.

Everything was in the same uncomfortable, untidy way—cups and saucers, and glasses greasy, cracked, and dirty. The carpet covered sundry holes in the floor, the blinds would neither move one way nor another, the curtains were gaudy rags of blue and yellow. All was comfortless but the turf fire. My bed-room opened out of the sitting-room. I did not, however, inspect it. I dare not—for I felt that ignorance was bliss, and I accordingly took off my clothes by the fire, and putting out my candle, made a plunge into bed, and soon fell asleep. And well it was I did so, for when I arose in the morning, there was sufficient around me not only to have prevented repose, but to have deterred me from going to bed at all.

Gladly did I set forth with the early dawn, and after clearing the squalid and filthy purlieus of the town, the soft balmy air that now blew from the west was delicious and refreshing. I could not help speculating, as I went along, how it was that this fertile island should he so neglected, and the inhabitants so lazy and so dirty in their habits,—for as I passed hastily through the town, creatures only half human were seen crawling about the doors, and steaming heaps of dung were conspicuous before many a threshold. It only shows to what a state of endurance and misery man can be reduced, and yet live!

My road lay now among bogs, partially reclaimed, owing to their contiguity to the town. I then climbed an isolated hill, from the summit of which my eyes ranged over the very barony or district where my father's newly-acquired property was situated. As I looked I shuddered. Below me, stretching far to the westward, was a huge flat bog, reaching on the right to an arm of the sea, bounded on the north by lofty mountains; on the left it stretched far away southward, being again bounded by a similar lofty range. It was indeed a scene of utter desolation. Here and there some poor creatures had erected a cabin of turf and stones, and brought a few strips of land around it into a state of half-cultivation.

A few geese, a donkey, and one or two diminutive half-starved cows, were seen rambling around the precincts in search of what they could scarcely find—a nibble of sweet grass. Numerous holes, where turf had been dug out, now half filled with water, and an occasional rick of this useful fuel, were the only variations on the surface, if we except here and there a stream, black as ink, which forced its way deep through the spongy mass.

I looked back and felt a strong inclination to make a run for England—but my father was a man not to be trifled with, and he had served his country too long not to have confirmed the habit of expecting implicit obedience. Five thousand pounds! "Why," thought I, "a tithe of the sum ought to have purchased the whole barony." Sorely did I blame my own rashness for so hastily consenting thus to banish myself from comfort, civilization, and refinement. However, there was no help for it now, and so I e'en pushed on in no very amiable mood.

The public road crossed the bog, and after traversing it about a mile, I took a by-road to the left, which, as I was informed, would lead me to Rathlynn. As I proceeded, cabins, such as I have described, increased in number, but all exhibiting the same squalid wretchedness. I met a gentleman's servant (cheering sight) driving a jaunting car, and he informed me that these dwellings were inhabited by "farmers," some of whom were "snug enough." He also said that the first turn to the right near the school-house would bring me soon to my destination.

Pedestrianism in Ireland is weary, dreary work, and I began entirely to agree with Mr. Stamer as to the comfort and advantages of a conveyance. No portion of the country

I had hitherto seen was desirable to walk over, and as for distances, there seems no end to an Irish mile. But see, there is the school-house, a tall, stone-built, whitewashed building, having the windows protected with a network of wire, a sure proof of the mischievous propensities of the urchins therein "educated." It is, I suppose, the breakfast hour, for now they are pouring forth from the portal, running, and shouting, and leaping like so many imps. They have caught a donkey, three are on its back, two seize the tail, and others are tickling the poor creature's flanks with rods of prickly gorse; it places its head between its legs, and with one kick floors at once five of its tormentors. A loud shout and cheers from the others, but no one is hurt—they are on its back again, and in vain does it gallop, or kick, or plunge, the tormentors are still there, and there is no shaking them off. I thought I had never seen anything like the activity of these wild gorsoons in my own country. It was marvellous.

Here there were two roads—the one to the left, and the other to the right. I took the former as being the widest, and travelled on, passing first over a barren mountain, then skirting a succession of small, dreary looking lakes, then descending into a wide valley, all bog and morass, where the road all at once failed me, having been made only thus far and no further. It was now past noon, and heavy clouds hung on the mountains, and gradually descending lower and lower, portended a storm, which ere long burst over my head. I ran for shelter to a cabin that was on the verge of the morass, and entering, found it was deserted. A portion of the thatch had been removed, and the rafters, black as ebony with smoke, swung to and fro in the blast. The place had not long been untenanted, for the ashes of a turf fire were still on the hearth. And why had the place been thus deserted. There were three usual causes in this miserable country—America, the poor-house, or the fever! In one corner was a remnant of a wretched bed of straw, and a broken cup containing some water was placed near it. It was fever! What so likely near a wet spungy expanse, such as was spread out before the spot for full half-a-mile? Though it rained in torrents, I fled the place, and, again taking the road I had left, I retraced it for some distance without seeing any signs of human habitation. At length I arrived near the top of the mountain I had recently crossed, and there, among enormous masses of huge boulders, I found a kind of natural cave, in which, as the storm was increasing in fury, I found a rude shelter till it again passed away. But this was not till the sun had long set; and I resumed my journey, conscious that I had taken the wrong road, and wandered miles away from the place of my destination. Not one human being did I meet till I regained the school-house, where I was informed by the master that Rathlynn was only one mile distant on the road I ought to have taken. Such are the effects of having neither mile-stones nor yet sign-posts to direct the traveller.

It was now quite dark, and heavy clouds obscured the light of a young moon, which once or twice was visible for a moment, as the seceding vapours were occasionally divided by the hurrying tempest. At length I reached Rathlynn. A pair of rusty iron gates, affixed to piers huge and rude, and out of all proportion, received their new owner; but one half the gate was down, the other swung on one hinge, making hoarse music with the blast.

Passing along a road, rough with stones and deep ruts, I at length gained the house, and congratulated myself in the prospect, at least, of a comfortable shelter. A comfortable shelter? We shall see. A tall man, with an uncombed head of fiery red hair, somewhat past middle age, and with a countenance seared and furrowed by excessive hardship, or by want, or by intemperance, or by all three, opened the door, and, on my giving my name, preceded me into the kitchen (so called), for there was no fire, he said, in the house, but there. The kitchen! The walls were stained with dirt and grease, the ceiling was blackened with smoke, the earthen floor full of pitfalls and water traps for the unwary. A bench, two old crazy rush-chairs, and a rickety table were all the furniture. Two iron pots, a griddle, and a little cracked and discoloured crockery, of the commonest kind, made up the sum total of all ostensible culinary articles.

"And this is Rathlynn, the place Admiral Wyville, my respected father, has purchased?"

"Surely," replied the savage, looking surly.

"I only wish, then," said I, incautiously, and smarting under my disappointment, "that my father had seen the place before he had anything to do with it."

"Better men than your father or yourself have lived here, and been well satisfied," rejoined the man, at the same time heaping up the fire with fresh turf. Once more I looked round despondingly, but felt that quietness and resignation, and even civility, were necessary in my somewhat equivocal position. I accordingly stripped off my waterproofs, which, luckily, I had brought with me, and, closing to the fire, determined to make the best of it. By-and-bye a stout, coarse-looking girl with bare legs, and a scanty costume that had never known the washing-tub, made her appearance, and preparation for supper was commenced. Soon half a smoked salmon and a tray of unpeeled potatoes were on the board, and though the fish had been what they call a "spent salmon"—that is a fish out of season, returning to the sea after spawning—I ventured to taste a small portion of it, though the principal part of my supper consisted of a bowl of butter-milk and the potatoes aforesaid.

After these were removed, and a pitcher of whisky-punch substituted, my host became more conversable; told me I was not expected for a week, and made a sort of apology that he had not had a fire in the parlour for my separate accommodation. He said my bed was well aired, for the girl had slept in it herself the night previous. I felt a cold chill run over me at this agreeable announcement, and I at once expressed a wish to see my apartment.

The girl preceded me up a flight of stone steps, dirty with the leavings of fowls, and, as I fancied, of goats also, for the smell was close and sickening. The banisters were gone. We passed along a kind of long corridor, into which several doors opened, and at the termination of this I found myself in my bed-room.

Half the ceiling was broken in, and long pieces of lath and plaster were pendant therefrom; there had been shutters to the windows, but they were gone, and several panes were broken and pasted over with dirty brown paper. The bed!—the long and short of it was, I determined to remain up all night by the kitchen fire, and to get what rest I could by the aid of the bench and two chairs. I told my host on my return that I was so cold and wet that I preferred drying my clothes by the fire to going to bed at once; he was therefore at liberty to retire whenever he felt inclined. The girl, after bringing in a fresh supply of fuel, disappeared, and her master very soon afterwards retired, leaving me to the enjoyment of my own reflections.

And was this Ireland—the first gem of the sea?

To me it appeared altogether a dirty, disagreeable country. Nature had perhaps done something—art and industry nothing.

I fell asleep, indulging in various speculations, and as the fire was still burning when I awoke in the morning, and the room was warm, I did not, after all, experience so much discomfort. The window of the kitchen opened into an enclosed yard, and so having made my ablutions, I sat down to a breakfast of eggs and coffee, with brown bread and bad butter, before I set out on a tour of observation.

My first object was to ascertain the state of the house, and accordingly I entered what was called the parlour, which was of a good size, with a bow-window. I stepped forward, and gazed upon the prospect before me. I was at once struck with astonishment and admiration! The morning was fine, and the rising sun illuminated the landscape. It was a glorious, gorgeous sight! The house was situated on a gentle eminence, rising from a lake, which, like a mirror, reposed calmly and quietly in the bosom of the mountains. The shores were rocky, and in many places feathered with underwood. The width of this large expanse of water might be a mile and a half, and looking southward from the window where I stood, about three or four miles, it was seen to curve round a wooded promontory, losing itself in the mountain gorges beyond. On the south-eastern shore rose a vast range of rocky mountains, throwing up two or three peaks into the clouds, and these again were separated by deep gullies, hemmed in by perpendicular rocks, down which, owing to the heavy rains of the preceding day, numberless cataracts were pouring in silver threads. Far again to the south, peering over a succession of lower ridges, were visible the broken and fantastic summits of the Glenhara mountains, through which no roads had yet been made, and which, to all but the scanty population around them, were a perfect terra incognita. The immediate borders of the lake were highly picturesque, and, like a bold and varied framework, enclosed the now still and gleaming mirror, as if on every side—though, on examining more narrowly, a slight bend to the far southward intimated that the waters forced their way further into the interior of the mountains.

I stood entranced. Never before had my eyes been feasted with such a prospect as this, and I could not help thinking my wanderings of the preceding day had been fortunate, as thereby the whole of this magnificent panorama burst upon me suddenly and unawares. The discomforts I had endured, the squalidness of the house I was in, were all forgotten, and I was long, very long, ere I could move from the spot where I had been so fascinated and surprised.

CHAPTER III.

"You may buy land now as cheap as stinking mackerel."
Henry IV. (1st Part).

In a few days I had pretty well realised my actual position, and exerted myself to meet its peculiarities. Mr. Ryan, the late proprietor, left the day following my arrival, taking with him his poor Irish slave of a girl, and the few goods and chattels he had in the world, but what was his destination he did not choose to impart—though I was afterwards informed that he had a small estate in Sligo county, to which he retired. It was manifest that he looked upon me as an interloper, and thought it the height of injustice that his estate should be sold to pay his long-standing debts. On examination I found the house and premises in a thorough state of dilapidation; besides the kitchen, one room only was weather-tight and habitable. I got the best specimen of a servant I could, and that was bad enough, from the neighbouring town—had the room and kitchen scrubbed, and scraped, and whitewashed, and I sent to Londonderry for a good bed, and the requisite furniture and articles of culinary use, and ere a week elapsed found myself in comparative comfort.

The chimneys smoked, as they usually do in Ireland, but by the application of a register grate and chimney pots, that insufferable nuisance was considerably abated. The exterior of the house itself, particularly as seen from the lake, was somewhat striking

—the windows of the lower story were large, and opened upon the terrace, and lofty dormers broke the uniformity of the roof. It had been a respectable dwelling at some period, but Mr. Ryan had certainly converted it into little better than a pig-stye. Wherever you turned was neglect, dirt, and ruin. Not a door was well on its hinges, not a casement without broken panes, the floor of the kitchen was in deep puddle-holes, and the smoke which pervaded the whole dwelling had tinged the walls and ceilings, and caused long dark stripes to disfigure the plaster wherever the rain or damp found an entrance.

I was not long in coming to the conclusion that the whole must be gradually taken to pieces and renewed, and I wrote to the Admiral requesting his permission to commence operations. The room I occupied being over the kitchen, and forming a kind of wing to the main body of the house, could easily be occupied, independently of the operations going forward. The precincts of the dwelling, or "premises," as they are usually called, were just as ruinous as the rest. The rain found its way into every outbuilding, and the rafters could be plainly discerned through many a hole in the slate or thatch. The only redeeming point was an immense turf rick, heaped up against the high wall, which, together with the outbuildings, enclosed the yard. For this I had paid Mr. Ryan double its real value, though it was totally unprotected by thatch, and was exposed to every shower that fell.

A garden so prolific, in one sense of the word, I never before saw. It was more than an acre, thick as an Indian jungle with weeds and brambles. Here and there a melancholy gooseberry or currant-bush might be seen struggling for life, and a few fruit-trees, gnawed and broken by the cattle, showed that here "a garden once had smiled." There had been walks and even beds of flowers, but all was now almost indistinguishable. The high bank that had once enclosed the place was trampled down in many places, and old pots and pans, broken crockery, and oyster shells were scattered everywhere, to my infinite disgust.

Certainly no Englishman could have endured such a state of things for a day, but I have since entered many Irish dwellings in no respect better than this, and inhabited too by persons who insist upon the affix of " esquire " to their names.

In the far west, at the time of which I am speaking, and probably for many centuries before, neatness, regularity, and order were things unknown. To live from hand to mouth, to make a " putting on " from day to day, to disregard dirt, damp, squalidness, and discomforts, to be indolent, careless, and unreflecting, were the characteristics of the people amongst whom I had come to dwell.

So busy had I been in trying to make my one room decent—in clearing the garden —in repairing the road to the house—putting up gates and mending fences, that, as yet, I had not had time to look over the estate. Indeed, it had been rainy, and I deferred it from day to day. Standing, as I often did, upon the narrow terrace which fronted the lake, I had observed to my left, on the eastern shore, a few chimneys rising out of a grove, and as the blue smoke often was seen gracefully curling up the side of the mountain that almost overhung it on the southward, I conceived it was inhabited by some respectable proprietor. Nor was I wrong. It was, I was informed, the residence of a Mr. Fitzpatrick, who had a considerable estate in the neighbourhood. Nor was he long in calling upon me. He was a tall, broad-chested, upright man in form, with greyish hair, thin and scattered in front, but falling behind over the coat collar almost upon his shoulders. He was dressed in a short grey jacket that barely covered his hips, with very ample waistcoat and trowsers of a light Scotch tweed, thick, laced boots, and a dark cap with a narrow gold band. He held, or rather grasped, a thick oaken stick, and a huge mastiff was at his heels.

"Egad, Mr. Wyville," said he, after the first hearty greeting was over, "my meaning is to call upon you, but as I know the devil of a room have you got to show a gentleman into, we will, if you please, make the terrace here into a drawing-room for the occasion."

With that he laughed heartily, and we

paced the terrace, as he declined entering the house.

"I often wonder," said he, "what can bring you English into these remote places. It is few Irishmen that would live in Donegal, if they had money enough to domicile in London, Paris, or Dublin. Have you looked over your lands yet?"

I confessed I had not.

"Well, then, you will find there is something for you to do. As for your tenants, they are a lazy, discontented set of vagabonds, and nothing but starvation and the strong hand of the law can keep them down."

"Starvation keep them down!" exclaimed I, in great surprise; "why, I have been always given to understand that poverty and wretchedness were the causes of these frequent outrages."

"Yes, and so you English think. In

your opinion, doubtless, unless a man has beef and pudding to his dinner every day, he will be, and ought to be a rebel. I tell you, sir, at once, and it may be a lesson to you as a new resident, that if you were to raise wages and to educate the people, they would seize the first opportunity of driving every landed proprietor out of the country. An Irishman's blood cannot run too thin in his veins."

Not wishing for any argument, I remained silent.

"Well, sir," continued he, after a long pause, "you must come to Mount Patrick, and see us. I shall be glad to have you as my guest, till you have got matters into some order here. We affect no style, but you will have a true Hibernian welcome—that I *can* promise you."

Seeing that he would take no denial, and fearing to commence my residence at Rathlynn by perhaps offending my nearest neighbour, I said that I would find my way to Mount Patrick the following morning, and have the pleasure of spending two or three days with him; more than that I could not spare, as there was so much to do at home, and the labourers, I found, needed continual personal superintendence.

"What," said he, laughing, "you have found that out already. Ay, and you'll discover more and more, every day you live, that England and Ireland are two very different places. I only wish all your bellowing English philanthropists would come and live here a twelvemonth, and they'd soon find out what a fruitless game "the amelioration of the Irish peasantry" is, and ever will be. I tell you, Mr. Wyville, it is not in them; as well teach the Hottentots or the Cape Bushmen."

After my new friend was gone, as the

morning was fine, I put on a strong pair of boots, and, with a long spud in hand, proceeded to examine "the estate."

As I left the gate and emerged upon the road, I met a tall, well-grown young fellow, who seemed loitering about with nothing to do. He made a low obeisance, and bade "my honour welcome" to Rathlynn. As he seemed both intelligent and civil I inquired if he knew the boundaries of the lands lately the property of Mr. Ryan.

"Sure," said he, "it's every mearing in the country I know right well, and it's every square *inch* of the lands I'll show your honour."

"Square inch," thought I, "an Englishman would have said every *acre*." I began already to have an inkling of the Hibernian style of expression.

My conductor, whose name I found was Dan McBride, executed his task well, and when I returned to the house, just as the sun was setting, I had made a cursory inspection of the whole estate.

To one accustomed to the well-fenced, well-cultivated fields of dear Old England, the face of matters at Rathlynn was far from encouraging. The lands which stretched along the north shore of the lake were altogether in grass, and were capable of supporting a large dairy; but they were almost in a state of nature. There had been once fences and a sub-division into fields, but they were so trampled down by the inroads of cattle as to be useless. Large boulders occasionally rose several feet above the surface; and where-ever a spring burst through the soil, there was a thick covering of rushes marking both its rise and progress through the lands. One glance, however, told me that all this was to be remedied, and that judicious draining and clearing would soon convert these now scanty pastures into rich and prolific meadows.

Leaving the shore of the lake the lands stretched northward for a mile and a half —a wild, dreary extent of bog and morass, except where a few patches of half-cultivated land surrounded a wretched cabin which was approached by a narrow "boreen," * often almost knee-deep in mire and dirt. It was just the sort of country I had wandered into before, when I lost my way. There were from thirty to forty of these small holdings, all paying a kind of *ad libitum* rent, and none having exactly ascertained boundaries. Many portions of the lands were flat and marshy, but here and there rose a low ridge or a conical hill, which generally were taken advantage of to screen the cabins from the violent west winds of the neighbouring coast.

* A lane.

On one of these natural mounds, or "escars," as they are called, Dan McBride and I stood, having before us a pretty good bird's eye view of the whole district. It was a cheerless prospect. The preceding rains had half deluged the country, and many a plashy bottom, and many a brown rushing torrent flowing from the neighbouring bogs, give an inconceivably uncomfortable aspect to the whole scene. All around were large patches of stunted heath and furze—in one place a plain covered with primeval rocks—in another a black extent of bog cut into deep holes by any chance comer who chose his own spot for cutting his winter's fuel.

"And so this is, or rather was, Mr Ryan's estate?" said I, in a tone of despondency.

"Yes," replied my guide; "this is the 'territory' of Rathlynn. And sure there are some snug farmers on it, as your honour may see; there's Mich McGrath down there, close to the bog water—he can walk the fair at Mullikeen with any man, and has three cows of his own, besides heifers and pigs. *His* rint is sure, anyhow."

"Then you don't think so meanly of the land, McBride?" said I, wishing to elicit his opinion.

"Meanly of the land?" re-echoed Dan, looking round sharply; "there's better land in Down and Antrim, they say, but if a man cannot be comfortable here, he'd better be off to America. Why, sir, this land will grow the finest taties in the whole country, and it's little of the rot we've ever had here."

"But," replied I, with an air of remonstrance, "the land is utterly ruined with stones and water."

"There is not a tenant but what has got an elegant tatie garden," rejoined McBride;

"and some have got a bit of Swedes, but that's a late invention. My father," continued he, taking off his cap, "is your honour's tenant, and we always pay the rint, and have plenty of milk to give the children, besides the meal and taties."

"Then you are quite satisfied?"

"Why not?—we have three quarters cow grass, and take three pigs and two heifers to the fair at Mullikeen every year."

It was very manifest that the tenants wished no change. They were well satisfied with the smoky hovel—the stony field—the plashy bog—and all the revolting accompaniments of Irish cottage life.

"But," said I, "if those marshy bottoms were drained and limed, and the stones removed to make fences for the land, and the furze and heath pared and burned, and the bogs cut on some regular plan, so as to drain without disfiguring and spoiling them, what do you think then, McBride?"

The poor fellow looked aghast at such a monstrous proposition.

"By Gor!" said he, "your honour's joking. Why, the whole County Cess could never do it. It would cost the whole territory over again."

"Not quite that," I replied. "Perhaps you do not know that some of our finest lands in England were originally no better than these. Like these lands, they were at first worth nothing, but by labour and manuring they now produce as fine crops as are in the world. I think this estate may be much improved."

Dan McBride gave no answer—the subject was manifestly beyond his comprehension. To spend money on the cultivation of land, was an idea which, in these parts at least, had never yet entered the head of a native. As I saw there must at least be something done, I at once hired Dan McBride as a labourer on the estate, a step I had never any reason to repent. He was ever sober, respectful, and, for an Irishman in Ireland, tolerably industrious.

CHAPTER IV.

"Believe me, lords, for flying at the brook, I saw no better sport these seven years' day."

Henry VI. (2nd Part).

It was a lovely morning when, according to my promise, I made my appearance at Mount Patrick, and received there, as its owner had predicted, a hearty welcome. I was introduced, in due form, to Miss and to Mr. Archibald Fitzpatrick, daughter and son of my host, with a notification that I should be made known to the lady of the house when we met at dinner.

"Well, Archie, my boy," said Mr. Fitzpatrick, addressing his son, what is to be the order of the day? Mr. Wyville does not expect to sit under a slate roof all the morning."

"The boat is ready, sir," said Mr. Archie, "and there is a fine ripple on the water. We will be sure to have sport. Mr. Wyville has sent down his tackle, I suppose?—if not, I can furnish him in our rough way."

I had luckily not forgotten my tackle, and felt some little pride in fancying how my regular outfit from Farlow's and from Kelly's would surpass the home-made articles of my new friends.

As yet, however, I was no adept in the piscatorial art, further than having, at long intervals, practised in my kind uncle's river at Penrhôs, and having caught trout, perch, and grayling in the quiet stream that meandered through my father's domain. I was, however, anxious to improve, and had spared no expense in furnishing my fly-books, and procuring the best rods, lines, &c., &c., as I had been informed the lake and neighbouring rivers abounded with fish, and that salmon of huge dimensions were occasionally to be met with.

As our boat glided swiftly over the smooth waters, my whole attention was absorbed by the splendid scenery which every fresh reach of the tortuous lake presented to our view. Sometimes the shores were bold, and almost perpendicular—cliff upon cliff, like another Babel, seeming to scale the very heavens. Then was seen a calm, sequestered vale, with its green patches of meadow, and its clear, rushing stream hurrying its petty contribution to the lake. And here was a small marshy plain, with a margin of reedy water, manifestly an encroachment on the wide extent, composed of the débris washed from the hills above, mixed with weeds and a decayed and decaying vegetation. And ever and anon, as we passed onward, were seen patches of natural wood, encircling, and sometimes half concealing the grey rocks; and above, stretching far away into the mountains, craggy slopes, covered with heath, where the goat and hardy sheep of the country were to be seen, enjoying their liberty, scanty as their fare might be.

Nor yet were these wild regions destitute of human habitation. Many a lowly cabin sent forth its blue smoke, high tapering above its sheltering trees or rocks; with its small patches of cultivated ground around it—the potato garden, the little meadow, the few ridges of oats, enough, and only just enough, to supply—we may not say, to satisfy—the wants of the simple, primitive inmates of these remote, and almost inaccessible abodes of humanity. And still, at a distance, how pretty, and how sequestered, and how sheltered and comfortable they appeared! Approach them not, traveller—the spell would assuredly be broken.

It was early in March, but the wind was from the west, and an air of freshness had begun to steal over the scene. Wherever a mountain streamlet trickled down, there was a long strip of the brightest verdure, and though the woods still wore the desolate garb of winter, yet in many a warm nook the birches had begun to put forth their infant leaves, and bunches of primroses in wild profusion—and they are peculiarly large and beautiful in these regions—already spangled the more sheltered bases of the overhanging rocks.

On, on we went, from the Lower to the Middle, from the Middle to the Upper

Lough—all one vast sheet of water, but each having the appearance of a separate lake, hemmed in by its own rocks and mountains. Each, too, had its distinctive features. The shore of the Lower Lough was most conspicuous to the north, on which both Rathlynn and Mount Patrick were situated. It was a low ridge, abruptly rising from the water's edge, but here and there broken into little verdant valleys, grazed by cattle and studded with trees of considerable growth. Beyond this ridge of cultivated land was the wild tract I have already mentioned — a huge extent of mingled bog and moorland, with occasional patches of cultivation. This stretched two miles or more, to the shores of Kilcullen Bay, on the other or northern side of which rose that magnificent range of mountains, also already alluded to, and which, seen from the lake, reminded one forcibly, though in diminished grandeur, of that vast panorama of the Pyrenees, which is seen from the lowlands of Navarre and Gascony.

But I will reserve further description to another opportunity, for just as we emerged from the Lower Lough, where cliffs almost perpendicular overhung a deep pool, a heavy fish rose at Archibald Fitzpatrick's fly, and, whir-r-r! away he went at railway speed, bending the end of the twenty-feet rod almost to the surface of the water.

"Hurrah for the wren's hackle!" cried Archie, turning for a moment to his father. "I told you, sir, it would beat your black hackle and purple body altogether and entirely. Now," said he, addressing me, and handing me the rod—"now, Mr. Wyville, you shall play the fish, and if you land him, won't it be a lucky beginning, and a bowl of whisky punch for the boys?"

I took the rod, but I felt myself tremble from head to foot, lest I should expose my ignorance and lose the fish. He had now reached the bottom, and there he lay like a sulky pig that he was, and I thought to move him by a gentle pressure of the line.

"Mind what you are about," said Mr. Fitzpatrick, who had now moved to my side; "he's a twenty-pounder by his roll in the water, and, egad! he'll run away with the boat before we've done with him. Keep a good hand upon him—so—that will do; when he makes off, let him go as far as he will, only keep the command, and have him well in hand; don't let him have his own way, my boy, or he's lost."

It was ten minutes before the fish moved —when he did, he showed that he was no sluggard. Off he went at railway speed, taking with him upwards of fifty yards of line. I began to enjoy and warm with the sport.

"Well done, young Sassenach," said my host, patting my shoulder; "you have a steady fist of your own, and that's half the game after all. Now reel him gently up—don't let him take his breath, the vagabond! Gently—gently—that will do."

Just at this moment the salmon (for such it was) made a sudden rush towards the boat, and my line became slackened.

"Wind up quick!—keep his head in the right place!" said Mr. Fitzpatrick; "and if he makes a turn of it, let him go."

And a turn indeed he did make of it in his own way, for before I could get him again fairly in hand, he suddenly rose to the surface, leaped at least a foot out of the water, exerting all his force to free himself from the hook firmly fastened in his gills.

"Sure he's after wishing us a good morning, and better sport elsewhere," said one of the rowers; "by Gor, he's gone, worse luck!"

But it was not so—the hook was too firmly fixed, and down he went again to the bottom, and I now had him well in hand. It was manifest the fish was somewhat exhausted, the boat was therefore impelled gently, and finding he made no resistance I again, under the direction of my friends, began to reel him up. He had now not more than fifteen yards of line, when, as if recovering himself suddenly, he again made for the surface, and commenced a struggle that caused my heart to beat and the blood to forsake my cheeks.

"This is the last dying speech and confession," said Archibald; "keep a good hand upon him—he must not show his tail or we are beat—there!—good!—good! down he goes again!—now wind up quick he's getting as weak as a kitten."

Twenty-two minutes by Mr. Fitzpatrick's watch were consumed before we could gaff our prey—and a prize, indeed, he proved—a salmon fresh from the sea, and weighing, as we found afterwards, eleven pounds and three ounces. From that moment I became a devoted fisherman, and under the instructions of Larry Lanigan, of whom more hereafter, there were few men in the county that could show such an array of flies and tackle, and knew better how to use them than myself. What child's sport does our English trout-fishing seem after one successful bout with a fresh salmon!

CHAPTER V.

"Ah, that deceit should steal such gentle shapes!"
Richard III.

I HAD only intended to spend one, or, at the most, two days with my new friends, but they so vehemently opposed my return to Rathlynn, that a week had elapsed ere I could venture to renew the subject. I was much charmed with their easy and profuse hospitality—they at once made me feel at home, and I was suffered to amuse myself just as I pleased, either in their society or alone.

"This is Liberty Hall, my young friend," said Mr. Fitzpatrick, slapping my shoulder in his usual hearty manner; "while you stay amongst us you are your own master; no questions are asked, and of course no answers required. It is enough for us if you feel at home."

And yet, to me all wore a foreign air—the manners, the feelings, the habits, were different from what I had been accustomed to. There was heartiness of manner — a readiness to oblige — and a kind of politeness, which sometimes approached formality—but, and I could scarcely explain why, it was not England, nor like it. In the general menage there was a clumsy inconsistency — profusion without luxury — and display without either neatness or order. I could detect cracks in the decanters—holes in the linen—stains on the carpets—and fractures in the furniture. Everything seemed to be left to take care of itself, and accidents might be deplored at the moment, but were seldom, if ever repaired. Locks without keys—bells without pulls, or pulls without bells—doors that stuck, and sashes that rattled. These failures were the rule of the house — no one regarded them — no one took the trouble to have them rectified.

And still, to the outward view, all was smart and showy. There were curtains of damask—chairs of walnut—and tables inlaid; gaudy carpets and china vases. The footman was in a blue and yellow livery, with long tags from his shoulder, and would have passed muster very well, but for that unlucky rent under his arm, which betrayed a shirt creditable neither as to texture nor cleanliness. Then there was no regularity. Breakfast was an *ad libitum* meal, and Dolan, the footman, had to change plates and to make tea just as often as suited the convenience of any of the inmates; and often did I pity the poor cook, who never knew within an hour or more at what time the dinner would be required to be sent up. Still every one was at his ease, and each went his own way. There was an apparent heartiness about Mr. Fitzpatrick that banished all restraint, and made you feel that your presence there could, and did, indeed, make little or no difference to any-one.

Archibald and I were soon sworn friends. He pioneered me over the country—showed me the best fishing pools—gave me some of his crack flies—allowed me frequently to play the salmon that he had hooked, and I set him down as a chip of the old block, and, like his father, open, courteous, and sincere.

As, however, the first reserve of our acquaintance somewhat wore off, I perceived that he was far from well educated; indeed, that he despised learning—that ardour and skill in the various sports of field and flood formed his estimate of a man and a gentleman, and that he had rather draw a badger, or hunt an otter, than improve his mind by reading, or his taste by attention to the fine arts. In fact, he was one of a race that we may hope will soon be extinct—the Irish "squireen,"—a man whose chief bliss was in a kennel, and who seemed to live for no other end than the gratification of every wild and irregular propensity.

I was some time, however, in discovering all this; indeed, my own thorough enjoyment of the wild sports of the West, after a three years' residence in college, was so great, that I could not have met with a companion more suited, for the moment, to my tastes and inclination.

Young Fitzpatrick was tall, handsome,

and remarkably active; his complexion was light, his manner joyous and excitable. He was expert in all manly exercises—fearless and daring. Like many young Irishmen of his rank, he was assuming, and haughty to his inferiors—exacting services which were most unreasonable, and never thinking any return necessary.

"Was it not enough that *I* asked him?" replied he to a gentle remonstrance on my part, when a poor half-starved gossoon brought a dog back that had been lost far away in the Glenlara mountains, and who received not even a thank-you for his fatigue and trouble. "Was it not enough that I asked him?"

It will be expected, probably, that I should say something of the daughter. Florence Fitzpatrick was both in mind and feature unlike her brother. She had a profusion of jet black hair—had dark eyes

—and her complexion was a clear healthy brown. Her features were good and regular — her manners quiet and retiring, though haughty, yet, when you observed her closer, there was sometimes a restless glance of the eye, and a rapid change of expression in her countenance, which did not agree with the general external calm.

"Florence is very like what her grandmother was at her years," said Mr Fitzpatrick to me, one day, when I had vainly importuned her to accompany us in an excursion up the lake. "She is a true Milesian. Her dark features—her proud step —her haughty reserve, are all of Spanish stamp. You must not be offended with her, Mr. Wyville; you will get on better by-and-by. She is a good girl, and can be amusing, too, when you know her."

I was willing to take it for granted, and felt little inclination to break the ice by further attempts to gain her good-will. But I soon found that Miss Fitzpatrick was not one to be overlooked. She had, in fact, all the talent and information of the family—was much made of, and her opinions were seldom contradicted. If she spoke, it was always to the purpose, and for her to approve or disapprove was, in all internal matters, law. Her mother was a person of no peculiar character—had been handsome—was proud of her husband and children—all-indulgent, and easily satisfied herself—in manner anxious and nervous. Her daughter, as Irish daughters often are, was uniformly kind and attentive to her, and though she had absolute rule in all domestic matters, contrived that it should be neither seen nor felt.

Such was the family at Mount Patrick, and in a short time I went in and out as if one of the party, and an intercourse of the most familiar kind was thus established between us.

Meanwhile I was not idle, but strained every nerve to reduce, if possible, our newly purchased property into some regularity as to management and appearance. The house, after a thorough cleansing—being also fresh plastered—rough-cast outside, and the roof repaired and re-slated—wore an entirely new aspect. I threw out a large window in the best parlour, which not only gave a recess of six feet additional, but displayed more favourably the indescribably fine landscape that lay before it. I added also a comfortable stable, and repaired the high massive walls that enclosed the yard at the rear. Other conveniences also, of various kinds, were not omitted, but which are too often deemed almost superfluous, even by the better grade of Irish proprietors.

"When the devil do you mean to stop?" said Mr. Fitzpatrick, one day, when, in his usual idle mood, he strayed up to see what I was doing; "you intend, I suppose, to astonish the natives. A little whitewash inside and out was all that was really required, and here you are routing the whole place about as if it had the plague or the fever in it. I suppose the admiral bleeds freely—but my rule is, when in Rome, do as the Romans do. There is a pretty round sum thrown away here, every farthing of which might be spared. You English are too extravagant."

"We are anxious to have things about us clean and comfortable, certainly," said I, laying down the hammer with which I was fastening a loose board in one of the floors.

"By the holies," said he, laughing, "I don't think you have any other word in your language but that. 'Comfort' is a part of every sentence an Englishman utters. A man is 'comfortable' in his circumstances, 'comfortable' in his mind, 'comfortable' in his house, in his family, in his person; has a 'comfortable' prospect or retrospect; is 'comfortable' in his neighbourhood, and in his servants; is 'comfortably' born, lives 'comfortably,' and dies 'comfortably.' My dear fellow, give me plenty to eat and to drink, a warm bed, and a slated house, and what can I want more? To my mind the Sassenachs are always working their wits to find out wants."

Nevertheless I persevered, and had the full benefit of my labours. No holes nor cracks let in the wind and rain — the chimneys ceased to smoke, and the doors and windows to rattle. The walls being mostly old and the weather fine and blowing, the plaster soon dried through, and ere the summer came, the dirty old mansion of the Ryans had become, for its size, the smartest lodge in the country.

But all this time I was not neglecting the land. Dan M'Bride, and one Mick Daly, were constituted regular hands, and they were my constant attendants on the lake and in the field. I soon discovered, as Mr. Stamer had told me, that to speak harshly to an Irishman does no good—a rebuke always hits hardest through a joke—and I learned so to adapt myself to the peculiarities of those around me, that everyone seemed glad to show me kindness, and my word was as good, in their estimation, as Dan said one day, "as a note of the National Bank." In the evenings, many were the books I read on agriculture, chemistry, and geology, with a wish to apply their principles to the improvement of the estate; and the "Reports of the Government Commissioners on the Reclamation of the Irish Bogs," was my constant study.

But I found that general rules cannot be successfully applied to all particular cases, and I had to use my own judgment with regard to drainage, dressings, &c.; and in many cases to purchase experience at a dear rate. Still I worked on, my fondest expectations being even far exceeded in some cases by the abundance of the crops, while in others a complete or partial failure gave acuteness to my observation, and full employment to my ingenuity. In fact, I began to love my mode of life—it brought with it health and peace, and a feeling that I was doing my duty; and when at the end of the year I made up my books, I found, notwithstanding a considerable outlay in improvements, that I should not have to trouble my father for more than the quarterly sum he had always allowed me.

The fertility of Irish land is surprising equally to English and Scotch settlers. It matters little what the geological formation may be, it is a most grateful soil. Nothing at first could exceed the dreary, desolate appearance of the lands of Rathlynn—no fences; wretched cabins, and a surface of bog—heath, dwarf furze, or coarse grass. No water was let off the lands by drainage, and plashy pools and stagnant ditches abounded.

One summer's work made a startling alteration for the better, and as the boulders, which cropped out everywhere, were raised and broken into materials for draining, and as quickly buried under ground, the surface water disappeared, the heath, the furze, and rushes died out, and a fresh herbage sprung up, and every progressive step at improvement, by its almost wonderful result, encouraged more and more outlay, with the certainty of a remunerative return.

There are many natural advantages on the west coast of Ireland, which are but scantily made use of by the natives. Coral sand and sea-weed abound, but seldom do we see it used on an *enlarged* scale; though, when amalgamated with the boggy soil, it produces large and remunerative crops. No man seems to use more than will afford the necessary supply of potatoes, and a few loads, drawn by a half-starved donkey, suffice for the usual agricultural operations of the small farmer. It does not seem to strike them that what answers so well on a small scale, would equally succeed in a larger operation, and so it is that many thousand acres of productive land lie idle, or are only used as affording a coarse and scanty herbage to a few miserable cattle.

As it is not my intention, however, to write a work on agriculture, or bog reclamation, I will satisfy myself with the few general remarks already made—concluding with the stale, often quoted, but, as applied to the Irish, most true admonition, "Oh! fortunatos nimium, sua si bona norint, agricolas!"

CHAPTER VI.

"What an equivocal companion is this!"
All's Well.

TIME passed on—summer was gone, and the rich tints of autumn already began to glow beneath the slanting rays of the western sun. New charms were thus added to the prospects around me, and I spent many delightful hours in exploring the numerous lovely glens and solitary recesses that opened upon the lake, or pierced the rocky range of the Glenlara mountains. I could not say with the poet—

"Mihi tarda fluunt, ingrataque tempora;"

but the very reverse—for time sped rapidly away, and I neither experienced *ennui* nor low spirits in these regions, though so far removed from all I knew or loved.

My sister was a good correspondent, and not only sent me regularly details of all occurrences at home, but also professed the liveliest interest in all that concerned myself and my doings, and the country in which I was self-banished; and even my father sometimes honoured me with a communication, written with all the stiffness and formality of a despatch.

I had now become a settled inhabitant of the district—knew most of the families, and was on a footing of kindness and familiarity with most of my poorer neighbours, and if I did not find them sufficiently truthful in our intercourse, and if they were too much given to the commission of certain little "venial sins," particularly in matters concerning the distinction between "meum and tuum," still there was a general exterior courtesy in their demeanour, and often an amusing quaintness and vivacity in their conversation that caused me to like them rather than otherwise. Indeed, we got on very well together. I was not always overlooking my labourers, and they received their wages as regularly as Saturday came round. In all cases of sickness, I did my utmost to alleviate suffering, and in matters of religion or politics, I was studiously indifferent and taciturn.

As I had now become a professed sportsman I struck up a sort of intimacy with one Larry Lanigan, a fellow who made a precarious living by attending gentlemen who came into the neighbourhood for a few days' sport, be it fishing, wild fowl, or grouse shooting. In fact it mattered little what it was, if Larry could only secure his two shillings per day, and a drop of whisky to boot. He was a little, weather-beaten, hardy figure, held his head erect, and strutted after you with the air of a bantam-cock. His countenance was lively and his feelings excitable, and as we walked he would rattle away with his wholesale gibberish, a kind of *patois* between Erse and English, not half of which I either could or wished to understand. His stories were generally exaggerated statements of what had happened in the country, or suspicions, or anathemas vented against any neighbour who invaded his province or interfered with his peculiar notions.

And still Larry was a good little fellow, and one who could, if he chose, introduce you to good sport. He never hesitated at any trouble or fatigue;—a kind of amphibious being, he thought as little of the water as his fellow-poacher, the otter, and if necessary would jump up to his chin in the lake or river, and, without a thought of changing his raiment, would appear next morning as well and fresh as ever. And as to this same raiment it had also its peculiarities. Larry had a way, when any dashing sportsmen came down, of making his appearance in a suit so indescribably and hopelessly wretched, that sympathy was at once awakened, and decent trowsers, waistcoats, and jackets were often clubbed together by the gentlemen, and presented to the "*artisté*" with an injunction that he should throw his old remnants on the next dung-heap. This caused Larry to present very often a somewhat ludicrous appearance—everything was too large for him—the waistcoat would reach to his knees, the coat to his heels, and the trowsers he turned up so as to give a double covering to the calf of his leg. The mixture of colours, too, was ludicrous enough, and the little fellow strutted about, when in his best, like the magpie in peacock's feathers.

As this kind of costume did not by any means accord with my ideas of propriety, I gave him a complete suit of frieze and fustian, made expressly for him, and I made it a condition, also, that he should reserve these for his particular attendance on me.

I have seen many anglers who thought themselves clever, but in throwing a fly against wind I never saw Larry's equal. It was wonderful how skilfully and well he would whip a deep pool, and give a general invitation to the fishy inhabitants to partake of the luxuries he had provided for them in the way of flies, and how, when he had struck a fine fresh salmon, he would leisurely and artistically play it till it was landed, faint and exhausted, on the sandy margin of the river, or on the green bank on which he stood.

"What made you a fisherman?" said I to him one day, after he had landed very cleverly a fish of twenty-one pounds weight.

"What made me a fisherman, is it? Let us sit down here, master, on the bank, and I'll tell you how it came about. Sure it was one fine morning in April that, passing Ned McGuigan's door, I saw his long rod leaning agin the thatch with two flies dangling from the casting line. The dropper, I remember, had a blue hackle. 'Where's Ned gone?' siz I, to a gossoon as was running the pigs out of the garden. 'It's up to Dick Kelly's he's gone,' siz he. 'And when will he be back?' siz I. 'I don't know,' siz he. 'Will it be long?' siz I. 'The divel a bit I can tell you,' siz he, 'but it may be evening any how.' And so by dad the thought come across me, and I walked off with the rod as soon as the boy had turned the corner, and up I went as far as yonder pool, where the river makes a bend under the hill. Your honour can see the place just off to the left there. Well, I made a few casts with my line, and me never expecting anything at all, at all—when, solch! up comes a salmon like a devouring lion, and runs away with the blue hackle as if the divil was at his tail. By all the saints and martyrs, didn't I tremble with fright from the hair of my head to my very toes! 'Hurrah!' off he goes, forty feet of line and more, then right round the corner of that big stone that sticks up in the water like old Paddy Foley's bald head. I reeled up quick, and crept quietly below the rock, when off he went again into the deep water, where he worked himself into a passion, till I thought every minute he was gone. However, I stuck by him, for he was well hooked, and could not wriggle out of it, till I was tired out altogether. My head began to turn round, and I hardly knew where I was. At last I suppose he was as sick of it as I was. I drew him to the side, and fainted away entirely. Sure then, in due course I awoke again, and, by dad, what was there lying dead at my side, but a fresh river fish that weighed fourteen pounds two ounces!"

"Well, Larry," said I, "that was great luck, and it made you a *great* sportsman, I suppose?"

"From that day to this, master, I've never looked behint me. I sold the fish at Mullikeen for a one pound note and a shilling, and that helped me well to get tackle of my own. So this is the beginning and the end of the story, master, neither more nor less—God bless you!"

Well, many a pleasant day had Larry and I had together—many a salmon and many a big trout did we lure from their quiet haunts. Often would we kindle a turf fire in some sheltered nook of the rocks, or some umbrageous retreat in the woods, and enjoy a repast such as a metropolitan club could not boast. For hours reclining with my dogs around me, while Larry was fishing from the shore, or gathering wild flowers for my hortus siccus, did I enjoy some favourite author, or even sometimes perpetrate some original composition of my own.

Our commerce with Nature ever improves, refines, exhilarates; commerce with mankind too often ends, if it does not begin, with trouble and discomfort. I found it so. My happiest days in Ireland were those which I spent alone, or in company with my humble companions. I trod the heather with buoyant step, and my thoughts, like my actions, were free and uncontrolled.

But I was not doomed thus to enjoy myself very long. However quiet a young man may wish to be, some one will ferret him out—will encircle him with the world's net—will draw him, willing or not, into the seething ocean of social perplexities. 'Tis true I saw the Fitzpatricks occasionally, and frequently joined Archibald in a row up the lake or a stroll down the river, but I found Florence still cold and constrained in her manner, and had no inclination to foster any closer intimacy. She was a strange girl, and I often suspected was not quite the icicle people were inclined to suppose. An event, however, occurred, which, as the prelude to an important era in my life, I will relate in another chapter.

"Thank you, Frank," said my uncle Rosse, knocking the ashes out of his meerschaum, "that will do for one reading. Your description of Ireland and the Irish brings to my mind those lines of Virgil in the Georgics—

> 'Speluncæ, vivique lacus, et frigida Tempe
> Non absunt—illic saltus, et lustra ferarum,
> Et patiens operum, exiguoque assueta juventus,'

and which I would loosely render thus—

> 'Here caverned rocks and shady vales abound,
> Here grassy glades within the woods are found.
> A patient race half till the grateful soil,
> Inured to hardship and unceasing toil.'

I don't dislike what you have already read to me, but as yet there is a dearth of incident. I like a writer who plunges *in medias res.* A very few words would comprise all you have hitherto told us: I went to Ireland, I repaired my house, I improved my land, and became a great sportsman."

"Julius Cæsar, sir," replied I, "summed up his adventures in three words, 'Veni, vidi, vici,'—but from those sprung his Commentaries."

"Very modest, indeed, to compare yourself with Julius Cæsar," said my uncle, laughing. "I approve, however, of your conduct so far in that strange country. There is good policy in staving off intimacies. Beware of that girl Florence Fitzpatrick—those shy creatures with dark eyes sometimes turn out very basilisks. My poor brother!—but it is a long story—I won't tell it you now. Howell has announced tea."

In a few evenings afterwards, by Mr. Rosse's invitation, I continued my narrative.

CHAPTER VII.

> "Ah, nature, a' thy shews an' forms
> To feeling, pensive hearts hae charms,
> Whether the summer kindly warms,
> Or winter howls in gusty storms."
>
> *Burns.*

THE weather had now become so settled and the atmosphere so mild and equable, that the Fitzpatricks proposed to get up a pic-nic party, and made it a matter of course that I should be one.

"We have arranged," said Archibald, "to fill four boats—yours and our own from this end of the Lough, and Mr. O'Toole's, of Mullahash, and Colonel D'Arcie of Doonore will join us, as we pass them on our way.

Bring something or nothing, Wyville—we shall provide enough for all."

Never did a more glorious sun rise in the east than on the morning appointed for this *fête champêtre.* The summer heats were gone, and there was a clear crispness in the atmosphere that seemed to brace the nerves and elevate the spirits. I sauntered leisurely along to join the party at the Mount, leaving Dan McBride and Mick Daly to bring my boat round to the pier and jetty, from whence we were to start.

There is between Rathlynn and the Mount, but nearer to the latter, a narrow glen, formed, probably, by the frequent overflow of the bogs above wearing away the surface. A brown stream trickled down it to the lake. This dingle is crossed by a rude plank, nearly concealed by the birches and alders that nestle in the hollow; but looking to the right, through an opening in the foliage, the Lough is distinctly visible, and its pebbly margin approaches within a few yards of the place. Here I paused for a moment, for the sound of voices arrested my attention, and looking down upon the shore I perceived Archibald and his sister standing on the margin of the water and in earnest conversation. On his part no little excitement was visible, but she stood confronting him, calm, composed, and dignified, as was her wont.

I was hurrying forward, unwilling to be a listener, when I heard her say, distinctly,—

"Archie, I certainly will, and you know I am not easily frightened from my purpose."

"If you dare!" responded he, laying a peculiarly hoarse emphasis on the last word.

"Dare!" repeated she, in a still calm, but thrilling accent; "as addressed to me you well know that word has no meaning."

As I mounted the opposite bank I saw her

slowly returning towards the house, while her brother stood as in silent abstraction on the margin of the clear, still water. It is not in my nature to be very curious, or to trouble myself much in the concerns of other people, but there was a something so striking in what I had heard and witnessed, arising, perhaps, not so much from the language as from the manners of the speakers, that I pondered as I went along what it could mean, for I had never before witnessed any approach to dissension of any kind between the brother and sister.

On approaching the pier I found all ready to embark—Mr. Fitzpatrick in boisterous spirits throwing out his squibs and jokes with that cunning twinkle in the corner of the eye, so peculiar to his class and nation, and arranging all the details with the decision of one well experienced in such matters.

Archibald and his sister had just arrived, and a few young ladies and gentlemen from Mullikeen, and Mrs. Fitzpatrick was there also, all anxiety about the hampers and the cloaks, the umbrellas and parasols, and other conveniences necessary to the success of a pic-nic, even in a warm day in autumn.

"Easy now, Mrs. F. P.," said our leader, quietly handing his wife into my boat; "easy, I say—don't be after bothering yourself about these things. I'll do all that—just sit quiet, and look about you, and if you feel inclined to be 'giddy,'" laughing at his own joke, "nobody, dear, will accuse you of that in a general way—but if you *are* giddy, take hold of Mr. Wyville," laughing again, "and don't tumble into the water, my dear, by any means, if you can help it."

A grin from the assembled boatmen rewarded this sally, while I politely handed the lady into the stern of my boat, and seated her next to myself, I being steersman.

"Thank you, Mr. Wyville," said the lady, "I prefer the middle seat in the boat, as there will be less rocking—I am a very poor sailor, and anything but happy on the water."

"Florence, you will sit near your brother, with Miss Julia Corrigan," said her father, offering to hand her into the other boat.

"I prefer sitting next to my mother," replied she, placing her foot on the gunwale of my boat, as it lay alongside the pier.

I handed her in gallantly, and, as in duty bound, placed her in the seat just vacated by her mother.

"Thank you, Florence," called out Archibald, significantly, and looking very much out of humour. "I daresay we shall be quite as merry without you. If Wyville wants ice to his punch, and vinegar to his salad, he will have plenty aboard, anyhow."

Florence did not further notice this fraternal compliment than by a slight flush on her cheeks as she took her seat by my side, after arranging her mother's shawls and wraps so as to render her as comfortable as possible. This quiet act of attention to one generally so little thought of as Mrs. Fitzpatrick, by her own party, I could not but admire; indeed, Florence never failed in her respect towards her mother, though her manner to the other members of the family evinced but little interest or feeling.

"And now," shouted our leader, before he took his own place in his own boat, "are you all seated *comme il faut?* Let me see, Archie and Miss Julia—Dick Corrigan and Miss Juliet O'Flesk—Frank Wyville and

Florence Fitzpatrick—zounds, Tom Daly, what are you doing hugging close to your pretty sister Mary, take your place next to the lovely Miss Juliet, and let Gormon O'Flesk take your seat next to Mary. That will do—the turtle-doves are all mated, so now, boys, we will start. Mr. Wyville, we will go ahead, or those stout young fellows of yours will soon leave us far behind."

And two fine young fellows surely were Dan and Mick—broad-shouldered, active, and with fine open countenances, and with a reserve and propriety of manner truly pleasing. They were not your talking, canting, obsequious Paddies so common at all places of English resort, who call a Bristol or Manchester tradesman "my lord," or "the gineral," or "the colonel," or what not; and his equally delighted wife "my lady," and "your ladyship"—thus making large profits out of their vanity, while they, the said Paddies, are laughing heartily in their sleeves at the joke. So it was when I visited the Lakes of Killarney—the fellows persisted in calling me "Capting," because I looked like a "haro," and they swore I had been in "Inghia and the wars," and when we landed on Denis Island to lunch, they would call it by my name, and it should "be known by no other for ever and ever." And this nauseous folly can be listened to, and well rewarded also, by sensible men and women from the other island!

But we are now half way up the Lough, and have been joined by the D'Arcies of Doonore—the father a tall, military-looking man, his lady, once a beauty, and two sons, and three daughters, of a better stamp than usual. The two sons rowed the boat, a long, narrow kind of skiff, and Colonel D'Arcie was at the helm.

I do not profess to attempt long descriptions of scenery, else, as we passed along, there was abundant food for such a propensity. The Lough, as I have before said, had three divisions—the lower, middle, and upper—entirely differing in their character. The former I have described. We were now in the middle lake, having turned the point of an abrupt promontory, which, at a distance, seemed to be its termination. The scene now became comparatively contracted. The deep and still waters were hemmed in on every side with craggy mountains of considerable height. Here, vast heaps of loosened stones, mingled with large boulders, the débris of countless centuries, shelved from the mountain side to the very borders of the lake; there, a vast perpendicular crag advanced its grey, mossy front, sometimes bare and naked, sometimes clothed with ivy, or displaying from its fissures the mountain ash, the holly, or the dark yew. Far up these slopes the goats were grazing, and below, where patches of true emerald green enlivened the savage glen, the small sheep and cattle of the country might be seen in numerous flocks and herds, while here and there a solitary cottage sent up its blue smoke above some sheltering grove or patch of copse-wood.

"How would you like to spend your life in one of those farm-houses?" said Mrs. Fitzpatrick, addressing me, with a kind of shudder.

"It would depend upon my companion," replied I, intending to be gallant.

"There is not—there never was, the person in the world who could entice me to live in such a place as this," said the lady, again shuddering. "I am not romantic, Mr. Wyville—I have no delight in rocks and deep waters. Florence thinks she has, but it is because she reads so much poetry, I suppose."

"My dear mother," said Florence, smiling slightly, "my mere reading poetry or romances could not give me a real taste for such scenes as these we look upon. Mr. Wyville's condition of making such a seclusion as this his home, he well knows altogether bars the probability of it. Where is the person whose companionship could atone to a man for the many social privations he would have to endure in such a spot?"

"Then you think it impossible that in the affection and entire sympathy of any existing human being a man could spend his life happily in this secluded spot?"

"I do think it most improbable. I have not, it is true, seen much of the world or its inhabitants, and human character may be of a higher grade than I know of; but certainly, in my experience, I have never seen two beings whom I thought such seclusion as this would satisfy long."

"And why not?" I inquired, wishing to draw out this generally taciturn young lady.

"Because the general characteristic of the world, as far as I know it, is selfishness, which is totally at variance with that all-absorbing sentiment of affection for another which must be the foundation of such a state of life as you have been describing."

"Then you think that to find your own happiness in that of another is beyond the reach of humanity?"

"Of men, at any rate; there are women to whom this *is* possible."

She blushed as soon as she had uttered this sentiment, for the conclusion might not unfairly be inferred that she was herself one of these women. And looking steadily at her at this moment, I almost thought she was. She appeared thoughtful, and the conversation dropped.

And now, nearing the eastern shore, and laying to beneath a stupendous cliff, the eyrie of eagles, we brought out our most killing flies, and invited the finny denizens of these waters to supply their share to the coming feast. I hooked and landed a small salmon—lost a larger, by having given my rod to my fair companion, to play the fish—caught two white trout, and half-a-dozen small brown ditto. Florence at length succeeded in capturing a fine trout of nearly three pounds, and was, in consequence, in great good-humour, and inclined to be agreeable. And, indeed, when she unbent, she was most pleasing, and perhaps the contrast with her general manner assisted this, for to find a female, reserved with others, unreserved with you, is a distinction more flattering to most men than they are willing to allow.

I felt in high spirits, and during our stay in this middle portion of the Lough, we all thoroughly enjoyed ourselves. But now having had sport enough, and not wishing to fatigue the ladies, we rounded another promontory, and found ourselves in the upper lake. Here the view greatly expanded. On our left were the lofty peaks of the Glenlara mountains, and far to the south, as if tumbled about by some mighty convulsion, was seen the disrupted outline of the hills of Mockmoy. It was a wonderful combination of scenery, both beautiful and sublime, and such as I never saw before. On our right, the heights receded, and were now gay in their covering of purple heather, and gently sloping to the shore were lands partaking of such symptoms of cultivation as Celtic husbandry can exhibit.

We were now rowing rapidly, and our boatmen seemed warming into a contest who should first attain the head of the Lough, when Florence laid her hand on my arm, and begged we might proceed leisurely, and suffer the other boats to get ahead. To the elder lady this was a most acceptable move, for she already began to hide her face in her handkerchief, and give symptoms either of alarm or giddiness, or both.

"Archibald," said Florence, somewhat bitterly, "is wilful and obstinate—he allows no suggestions—takes no advice; were I in his boat, he would not relax his speed. I therefore selected this, knowing well the opposite qualities of our steersman."

She looked at me furtively, and smiled slightly. Surprised, and gratified, I bowed low, but did not venture a reply. My father's veto rose to my mind, and I determined to be cautious.

We had now attained the head of the lake, and near the shore, on both sides of us, large masses of tall reeds afforded a secure retreat for numerous kinds of wild-fowl. Wild-duck, teal, and widgeons flew along the placid surface of the Lough as the plashing of the oars disturbed them, and the coots and water-hens, seemingly disregardful of us, played, and dived, and fluttered, and skimmed along the waters.

The other boats were now considerably ahead, and leaving the lake we found ourselves in a deep and quiet river, which urged its languid course through flat banks on either side. We pursued this for about half a mile, when on our right the land began to rise gently—large masses of rock occasionally obtruded themselves—and the higher ground falling away somewhat from the margin of the river, was covered with large hollies, silver birch, and here and there a group of stunted oaks, throwing their arms about in every fantastic shape. It was a very wild spot—almost savage. As we passed slowly along, the bank became higher — the wood thicker — till at length an opening in the trees discovered a few chimneys behind a lofty fence of hollies, and a rude unmown lawn shelving down to the water's edge.

"Who lives there?" I inquired of Florence, as I saw her carefully scanning the spot, as if looking for some one; "often as I have passed by, I have never yet seen any inhabitant, nor can my men inform me who resides there."

She returned no answer, but, looking up the river and perceiving that the other boats were not in sight, she requested to be put on shore.

I proposed to accompany her, but she declined. On landing she hurried up a narrow path, and quickly disappeared in the wood. I said nothing, but looked at Mrs. Fitzpatrick.

"I know nothing at all about it, Mr. Wyville," said she, as if answering my silent appeal; "neither Florence nor Archie are in the habit of making me their confidante."

"But who lives there?" questioned I, feeling a new and strange curiosity to know.

"I cannot tell," replied she; "they call the place Ballybog, and that is all I know about it. I suppose some herd or care taker lives there, for there is smoke rising from the chimneys."

"Have you heard anything about it, boys," said I, addressing Dan and Mick.

"Nothing," said Dan, "beyont this, that a brother of Father Roche is the present tenant, your honour, and he's ailing, and never goes out."

"And how long has he been there?"

"Jeminee, sir! that's more than I can tell—Mick, do you know?"

"I know nothing and can say nothing," said Mick, looking serious; "nobody goes there, and they go to nobody's. Tim Nolan was out there nutting, and a young woman set a great dog at him, and Tim, in running away, broke his shin, and was laid up for a week, so since that nobody cares to be about the premises. Besides," continued Mick, looking at Dan McBride, "people do say——"

"Be dhe husth," * said Dan, in a low voice in Irish, shaking his head.

At this moment Florence was seen hastening down the path; her face was flushed, and she took her seat in the boat without making any remark. The boys seized their oars, and we dashed along to overtake the

* Hold your tongue.

others. There was something strange about the whole scene, but I felt it improper to press any further inquiries.

We had now neared the other boats, which were stopping about a mile above Ballybog, at a house on the right bank of the river, the residence, occasionally, of Julius O'Toole, Esq., or, as he loved to be called, "The O'Toole;" it had the euphonious name of "Mullahash." They were to be of the party, and a gentleman and lady, with two daughters and a son, were seen emerging from the front entrance. We had joined the other boats in time for the greetings, which were somewhat noisy, for Mr. O'Toole was as hearty and boisterous as an Irish gentleman ought to be. He was a little stout man with a round smooth face and ruddy complexion; had a smirk upon his countenance, and was much given to rubbing his hands together. He had a great deal of banter, and never omitted an opportunity of perpetrating a pun, which seldom, however, told, except for its absurdity. Mr. Titus O'Toole, the only son, and future representative of the family, was a young man very dissimilar to his worthy parent. He was tall, thin, and dark-visaged. His long lantern-jaws seldom relaxed into a smile, and his white starched neckcloth seemed as if it would choke him. He had just passed his first term at Trinity College, Dublin, and seemed to have a magnificent idea of his own importance. His speech was rare but sententious, and savouring more than it might otherwise have done of a strong brogue by the attempts he made to hide it. His sisters were O'Tooles all over, merry sparkling girls, with round figures, good-humoured faces, and exceedingly like each other. They were named Eleanor and

Emma, which Mr. O'Toole abbreviated into Nelly and Em.

We had only to row a short distance further, ere we entered a spacious and deep pool, into which the river flung itself over a sloping ledge of huge dark stones washed down from the mountains in high floods. Spanning the summit of this ledge was an ancient bridge of three arches, over which, in the blue distance, rose the peaked summit of the Knockmoy mountains. To describe the romantic beauty of this spot is impossible, nor shall I attempt it—the whole burst upon us with a suddenness that, for some moments, rendered us speechless—we were awed into silence.

As a considerable portion of the property around this spot was Mr. O'Toole's, he had fixed upon the place where we were to assemble, and in this showed very good taste. Running the boats against the clayey soil of a flat meadow, we followed our leader, and crossing a road, and passing a limekiln, we turned up the rocky heights to our left, and taking a footpath leading through the copse, at length gained the summit of a bold knoll, where we were ordered to halt.

Here was a natural lawn of velvet turf, sheltered on every side with large hollies and spreading oaks. Scattered around on the margin of this open space were sundry huge stones, raised into their position by Herculean labour, probably, in ages gone by, intended for refuge and defence, or perhaps for the performance of Druidical rites. The spot might have been made for the purpose to which it was now appropriated, and when we had all chosen our places, some on the ledges of the rock, some under the dark shade of a holly, some on the green turf, the scene was certainly picturesque and striking. In the centre was a fire of turf, the blue smoke ascending in a straight line into the calm clear sky above, while our boatmen were busy emptying the baskets, boiling the potatoes, and cooking the fish with pointed sticks made of the arbutus.

The occasional bursts of merriment broke strangely on the tranquil scene around, for there was not a cloud on the sky, nor one playful zephyr stirring the dense foliage of the woods. I had thrown myself on a mossy bank, somewhat retired from the rest of the party, that I might, unmolested, enjoy my own thoughts, and make my own observations, when Larry Lanigan stealthily approached behind me and whispered that "the mistress," to wit, Mrs. Fitzpatrick, wished to speak with me.

"And was it the mistress, Larry, that told you so?" said I, looking him steadily in the face.

"The mistress is it?" replied he, repeating my question, the usual Hibernian mode of gaining time. "Sure, was it the mistress, your honour said?"

"No, it was not I—it was you who named the mistress. Did *she* send you, Larry?"

"By the eleven! and who else, seeing she is sitting all alone by herself just on the edge of the big rock yonder."

And so Larry, quite satisfied with his own adroitness, and probably not wishing to be further interrogated, stole quietly away. I rose immediately and joined Mrs. Fitzpatrick. She was seated comfortably on a cushion, her back leaning against one of the large stones we have already mentioned.

"Will you do me a favour, Mr. Wyville?" said she, in a low tone. "I may tell you, in confidence, that Titus O'Toole admires Florence, and Florence detests *him*. But her father is bent on the match, and I fear there will be some uproar, which I particularly dislike. See, she has just turned from him, and is coming this way. Could you, dear sir, draw him away, and allow her to take her seat by me unmolested. He never speaks to her unless they are alone, and it is very seldom indeed she gives him the opportunity."

I was vexed—but what could I do? I bowed acquiescence, and approaching the fire I called to Mr. Titus to come and assist me in distributing the plates and knives and forks.

Without moving a muscle, he slowly raised his eyes in astonishment at the absurdity of such a request to the son of "The O'Toole," and turning round again to address his companion, he found she was gone. One look towards me, which said pretty plainly, "I won't forget this," and he slowly moved off to join his father, who was laughing and joking with the Miss D'Arcies.

Not wishing to rejoin Mrs. Fitzpatrick after this demonstration, I busily occupied myself in directing the men what to do, till Mr. Fitzpatrick himself interfered, and begged I would kindly take his wife under my charge, as he was so busily employed in arranging matters touching the coming refection. I obeyed, and as I approached, the lady made a place for me, and I found myself permanently seated between her and her daughter.

Ample as was the supply to the appetite, the feast for the eyes presented from this spot was not to be rivalled It commanded a complete panorama of the surrounding country. All around, far and near, were ranges of mountains, tossed into every fantastic formation—peaks, ridges, and precipices. Into many a deep and savage glen the broad beams of the sun were partially penetrating, while bogs, and woods, and heaths filled up the mighty picture! Our seat was on the verge of a precipice, feathered from its base to its summit with silver birch and mountain ash, holly and twisted oak, all growing from the fissures in the rocks, and now in full and luxuriant foliage—but so precipitous were these cliffs that the view was not obscured. Far, far below were seen the windings of the river Glynne, from its eastern source in the Glenlara mountains, till, approaching the precipice with a graceful bend, it threw its copious waters through the dark arches of the bridge, and foamed and fretted over the huge ledge of boulders we have already mentioned, till it was lost in the deep and silent pool where we effected our landing. From hence it stretched far away amid flat meadows and feeding grounds, till it joined the lake, the whole expanse of the upper portion of which was visible—a clear mirror in a gigantic framework of rugged and lofty mountains.

"Is not this glorious?" said I, addressing Florence, after a long interval of silent contemplation.

"Can it be otherwise, considering whose creation it is?" responded she, musingly. "And still, is it not strange, Mr. Wyville, that the petty cares and anxieties of life so mar our enjoyment of the lovely scenes in which Providence has placed us? I feel as if care would pursue us into Paradise."

"We are told not—and, after all, human annoyances are generally, in themselves, so trifling and so short that, gazing on such scenes as this, they may well be flung behind us and forgotten."

At this moment Mrs. Fitzpatrick was called away, and we were alone. I looked at my companion and perceived that she was more than usually pale—her dark eyelashes were closed upon their lids, and she seemed deeply absorbed in some subject wholly unconnected with the scene around her. At length she placed her hand upon my arm, and looking up with a languid smile, said abruptly,—

"I do not love mystery; may I ask you, did you overhear Archibald and me this morning as you stood near us on the bridge?"

"I was not aware you saw me," said I, evasively.

"I did see you, and you overheard us. I do not wish you to suppose that I spoke thus to my brother without a sufficient reason. It is strange how little amenable to reason are the human passions and affections."

I did not reply, but waited for some clue to this peroration.

"I do not know that I have any right to trouble you, Mr. Wyville, with our concerns, but, as a neighbour, I should not wish you to misunderstand us."

At this moment Mrs. Fitzpatrick was seen approaching, and she added in a low tone—

"I will contrive an opportunity of speaking with you by-and-by."

I own I felt flattered. At last this proud girl had relaxed, and certainly she had much improved in my opinion that day. Her usually calm, imperturbable features had more than once flushed up, and like the lurid gleams from the snow-clad summits of Hecla, disclosed the fires that glowed within. That she had a soul not devoid of sentiment, I was convinced, and that she had an aspiring intellect I had been aware from the first. "She would contrive an opportunity"—the words rung in my ears—it was like laying the foundation of future intimacy and mutual confidence.

It is a great stride towards nearer relations when anything passes between young persons of different sexes implying "contrivance," however innocent in itself. It is a false step in both, unless warranted by the circumstances of each party.

I felt it so, and a something whispered in my ear, "Beware!" One thought of my father, and the excitement of the moment passed away. I joined the D'Arcies, and conversed with the young ladies.

The luncheon being now at an end, a general dispersion was proposed, and forming various groups, each wandered away—some to the rocky valley, some to the bank of the river and the bridge, and some into the wild wood paths. To the former of these places I intended to accompany the

D'Arcies, and set out with them accordingly. Scarcely, however, had I gone fifty yards, ere Larry Lanigan, stepping out from behind a holly, intercepted me, and said in a whisper that Mr. Fitzpatrick wished to "spake with my honour." I wished Larry and Mr. Fitz at the bottom of the river—but what could I do? I returned to the spot, and there I found our leader in a thorough Hibernian passion, holding his clenched fist towards his son.

As I approached, Archie disappeared, and with him all signs of anger in the parent.

"Oh! Wyville—is it you? I wish you would kindly take Mrs. F. P. under your wing once more; she wishes to call at McCarty's cottage, and I must go with the O'Tooles as far as Mullahash, to see his new stables. Will you oblige me?"

I bowed an assent, not, I fear, with a

very good grace; but, without further speech or notice, he hurried away, and I found myself with Mrs. Fitzpatrick on my arm. The young lady, however, was gone, and so far was good. I did not dislike my companion—she had, it is true, little or no character in her composition, but she was always mild, kind, and unselfish.

Descending the hill, we crossed the bridge, and after a short walk up the road, found McCarty's house on the left hand, surrounded (an unusual thing in the west of Ireland) with the outbuildings and conveniences of various kinds. The farmer and his wife were well stricken in years; but in dress and manner they were superior to their class. They welcomed us warmly, and we were soon seated in their little parlour adjoining the kitchen, talking of old times, and of changes in the country.

"My grandfather," said the old man,

"can remember this country when it was all one great forest; oaks and hollies as old as the deluge were here, there, and everywhere, and they used to say that wolves and red deer were as plentiful here as hares and rabbits are now. Lord a' mercy! how the place is changed even since I knew it! When his honour, Mr. Grandy, came to the estate, the first thing I saw was all the fine trees marked and numbered with white paint, and then, when spring came, nothing was heard through the woods but the clang of axes, and the grating of saws, and the thunder of falling timber; and so it went on for years, till scarce a tree was left to show what the place had been. And then sprung up all these large woods of copse from the old stems, which make it so thick that no one can walk except in the worn paths, whereas, I remember, you could walk for miles in great groves, when the trees stood up as high and close as ship masts in a dock. Then behind here were once the great works where they smelted iron with the timber of these woods, and there one Sir John Riskett made a large fortune, and bought up a great part of this country, which his successors now enjoy, living far away, and doing no good."

I had heard before of this "bloomery," and as Mrs. Fitzpatrick pressed me to go and see where it once stood, while she sat and chatted with her old acquaintance, I at once sought the spot.

Passing through a meadow bordering on the lake, I saw before me the considerable remains of buildings, and, in particular, a tall gable covered with ivy, and which, with its connecting walls, seemed to have been a chapel. As I neared the spot, my attention was arrested by heaps of scoriæ, and remains of what I supposed were workshops and habitations. Long grass and ivy, and stunted trees, covered the whole place, and rendered these ruins invisible till you were actually on the spot.

For a few moments I stood and contemplated the scene before me—once the abode of busy toil, now a still and solitary wilderness! I passed on till I reached the northern end of the gabled building, and turning the corner suddenly I saw a figure seated on a portion of the outer wall. What was my surprise when I discovered that it was Miss Fitzpatrick! Wishing to withdraw, and hoping I had not been seen, I attempted to retreat, but she rose and beckoned me to take a seat beside her.

"I told you," said she, as I somewhat reluctantly obeyed, "that I would contrive an opportunity of speaking with you, for I feel it must be done."

I seated myself on the ruined wall, and

there was a long pause, as if neither was willing to break a silence that began to be awkward.

"I ought to apologise, Mr. Wyville," said she, at length, "for the liberty I have taken; but there are circumstances it may be well for you to know—as it may be in your power to assist us."

I bowed, and awaited the *dénoûement.*

"You must be aware that my brother is understood to be the accepted lover of Julia Corrigan. The match is very desirable to both families. Lately, however, my brother has not, indeed, drawn back—that he dare not do—but he has been almost indifferent, which has created a feeling of uneasiness among us. I have perceived the change, and not failed, also, to ascertain the cause. He is flirting with another—an unknown penniless girl. You inquired, as we passed, who inhabited the lone cottage on the lake where I called on leaving the boat. She lives there with her moon-stricken father, but who or what are their means, no one seems to know, but one Father Roche, who occasionally sees them, and has vouched for their being harmless and inoffensive. How and when Archibald gains access there I cannot discover—there is a mystery about the whole matter. When I charged him with this new attachment, this morning, he was furious, and when I told him I would see the girl myself and warn her, he dared me to do it, with looks I could not misunderstand. Nevertheless, as you saw, I *did* call, but in vain. I could see no one — nor make any one hear — the smoke, indeed, rose from the chimneys, but not a creature was to be seen."

She paused in violent agitation — her bosom heaved — her cheek was pale. I would not interrupt her, and she resumed:

"Now I know well that my brother has no intention of breaking with Julia Corrigan, and for very substantial reasons, but she has already suspected a change, and is acutely observant. She is a girl of spirit, and not one to be cajoled—I cannot enter into circumstances, but worse than pecuniary ruin would be the result, to my family, of any open rupture."

Almost breathless she paused again.

"I fear, Mr. Wyville, my anxiety carries me too far; but you will pardon an Irish girl if her feelings get somewhat the better of her discretion—you can assist us—you profess to be our friend—and, therefore, I have been thus open, and I appeal to your generosity to interfere."

"It is impossible!" replied I, warmly—for I saw a dangerous pitfall before me; "I cannot—dare not interfere in matters of this sort. Pardon me, Miss Fitzpatrick, desire anything else of me—but not this— —I could do no good."

Her dark eyes flashed, and rested on me for a moment.

"You dare not?—you could do no good? Then I have, indeed, acted foolishly—I did not know you. Be it so—I will say no more—I had, indeed, no right to count on your friendship—I cannot blame you, but still, I think, if you knew how important this matter is to us, you would not refuse to aid us."

"Nor do I," replied I, "so that I could be clear of undue interference; with this reservation you may command me."

"I do not know exactly," said she, musingly, "how matters stand, but this I do know, that Archibald is self-willed, and, in the pursuit of his own purposes, reckless of consequences to others. Would you not aid me in thwarting him in his designs? We may, I think, do it effectually without being discovered. I know, I feel," added she, regarding me with a look of the deepest anxiety and distress, "that I am not acting a feminine part—that you will condemn a manner and mode of proceeding so contrary to my usual habits and demeanour—but come what may, he shall *not* carry his point, and bring disgrace and ruin upon himself and us."

As this usually cold and haughty young lady thus addressed me, I felt my spirits sink and a kind of tremor come over me—a presentiment of evil possessed me, and I felt the meshes were entangling me, in spite of myself. I hesitated—I dared not trust myself to answer—I knew the danger and the inexpediency of such intimate relationship with a lovely woman. Yet, still I suspected no design beyond what she avowed. I believed her incapable of low cunning or complicity of any sort; the eloquence of her flashing eye, and the eagerness of her manner, were foreign to dissimulation—I was convinced her feelings were real, and from some cause or other, yet unexplained, the occasion was imminent.

A long pause ensued, and she seemed buried in her own thoughts. Her head rested upon her hand as she reclined against the higher wall that intersected the one upon which we sat. At last I felt it necessary to say something. I was uneasy in my position there—it was somewhat equivocal, and might, if noticed, give occasion to remark.

"If there is anything I can do, consistently with the reservation I have already made, you may depend upon my services, Miss Fitzpatrick. But I really do not see how I can interfere—or, indeed, how interference of mine can produce anything but mischief. If, however, Archibald consults me, or if I can indirectly influence him, you may depend upon my using every effort to divert him from his pursuit. More than this I cannot promise."

"Which is just nothing," replied she, mournfully. "I do not blame your caution, Mr. Wyville—it is a national virtue, I believe. I fear I can offer no motive—no inducement to secure or tempt your co-operation," and here she looked so searchingly, yet so tenderly, as it were, into my very soul, that my heart beat and my eye fell beneath her glance; "my influence with you," continued she, "is, of course, so faint and powerless that I see all must devolve on myself, and that there is but one further favour I can ask of you, and that is—to forgive, and, if you can, to forget all that has now passed between us."

She rose, and was about to pass on, when voices close to us caused us both to start, and I could perceive she trembled and turned pale:

"Mr. Wyville—this is worse than all—for your sake—for mine—we must not be seen together—quick!—turn the angle of the building there, and hasten towards the lake, while I remain here and meet our visitors."

I obeyed, and plunged into a thicket, bending down lest I should be observed, and on gaining the margin of the lake, leisurely regained the road, with a view of joining one of the straggling parties on their return to the boats.

I did not feel quite at ease, and yet I could not detect any fault in myself, and if Miss Fitzpatrick had interested my feelings, and roused my curiosity more than was prudent, how could I help it? Was it not a proud thing to be singled out by one like her, to be her confidant—her coadjutor and her friend? But I could not bear to ponder on these matters—it is too much our nature to yield to present fascination, and cast behind us the cold suggestions of prudence.

I had already gained the landing place, but found no one there but a boatman left to guard the property lying about in every direction. Accordingly I walked leisurely up the road towards the bridge, in which direction I heard the sound of voices, and soon met the D'Arcies and the O'Flesks, with Mr. Titus O'Toole, all but the latter in high spirits. He appeared moody and dissatisfied, and manifestly somewhat surprised to meet me walking alone.

"Oh! where have you been, Mr. Wyville?" said Susan D'Arcie, a fair, plump, rosy, blue-eyed girl of seventeen. "We missed you all at once, and I had quite expected you were to be my companion in our walk. You don't know what you have missed—such beautiful rocks; and we saw two salmon rise in the river, did we not, Fanny? Where *did* you escape to, Mr. Wyville?"

"Indeed," replied I, gallantly, "you cannot use the word 'escape' on such an occasion—you should rather say, whither did the fates hurry me sorely against my will. Mrs. Fitzpatrick sent for me to accompany her to McCarty's, and of course I was bound to obey."

"Of course," repeated Miss Susan, jeeringly; "what a good young gentleman you are—it was quite English—few of our Irish beaux would have been so obedient. However, we had a very pleasant walk."

"Without me?" added I, laughing.

"Oh! yes—yes—yes—certainly," shouted

all the ladies; and so we went on joking and bantering till we reached the Druid's Mount, as we termed it.

Here all were now assembled, and preparations for tea were actively carried on. Two kettles hissed and boiled on the large turf fire, and cups and saucers and plates were scattered all around—on the huge boulders, and on the grass. As I did not wish to be again monopolised by Mrs. Fitzpatrick, I busied myself with the preparations for the repast, so sedulously that my former persecutor, Miss Susan, called out—

"How long is it, Mr. Wyville, since you were head waiter at the Shelborne Hotel?—see, Larry Lanigan is quite jealous of you."

"And sure I have rason to be, seeing how active the young master is," said Larry, looking very serious.

The general laugh was against me, so I quietly took my seat next to Miss Susan, who seemed well satisfied with the success of her manœuvre.

Mrs. Fitzpatrick and her daughter, and Miss Julia Corrigan, I observed, were seated together, and when Archibald arrived with his father, his sister beckoned to him, and resigned her seat next to Miss Julia. She joined the D'Arcies, and I found myself once more in her company. No glance, however, referred to what had passed—she talked with young D'Arcie, and appeared quite unconscious that I was even present. Who could it be that had disturbed us? I could form no idea—I only knew that she had ascended the hill with the O'Tooles.

Fickle as woman is an Irish sky. As we were fully enjoying ourselves, small clouds peeped over the mountain range to the south-west—I well knew they were the *avant-courriers* to a storm, and I pointed them out to Mr. Fitzpatrick. He saw the danger as well as I did, and great was the clatter of packing plates and dishes, and great the hurry of collecting shawls and wraps, and vast, too, was the bustle of gaining the boats, and selecting their seats, among the young ladies and gentlemen present, so that when I reached the place of embarkation I found that my own boat was already filled, and my place at the stern monopolised by Mr. Titus O'Toole, who had seated himself next to my former companion with unblushing impudence.

I was indignant—but hesitated a moment; —was it prudent to assert my rights, and thus publicly to imply a preference for Florence Fitzpatrick? But was I to pass by such an impudent attempt, and perhaps to be sneered at afterwards, if I suffered it to pass unnoticed?

"Mr. Titus O'Toole," said I to him, coolly, "this is my boat, and the seat you occupy is mine."

"There are other boats and other seats to be had," said he, the blood rising into his yellow cheeks.

"Am I to understand, then," said I, fixing upon him a look he could not misconstrue, "that you will persist in retaining that seat?"

"And suppose I do," said he in a hectoring tone, "who will prevent me?"

"*I* will," said I, and suiting the action to the word, I sprung into the boat, and but for Larry, who threw himself in the way, would have flung the young squireen into the water.

"Oh," said he, seeing matters were serious, "to be sure the boat is your own, and I am not going to be intruding myself, but I feel very much obliged to you, Mr. Wyville, for your politeness, and will some time have an opportunity of thanking you for it."

"When and where you please, Mr. Titus O'Toole," said I, with a sneer; "only go to your own boat, and save me the trouble of showing you the way."

It was but a moment that this scene was enacting, but poor Mrs. Fitzpatrick was seized with such a nervous tremor that salts and camphor julep—articles she was never without—were called into requisition before she regained some degree of composure. I took my seat at the helm near Florence, but she continued grave and thoughtful. The storm increased as we emerged into the lake —the rain poured down in torrents—and Mrs. Fitzpatrick having landed at Mr. D'Arcie's house, under a promise of being sent home in a covered car, I and my companion were alone, save the two boatmen, who were briskly plying their oars. I sat close to Florence, protecting her as well as I could with a large umbrella, which made our isolation more complete.

Yet for some time neither spoke. 'Tis true I felt on easier and more confidential terms with my fair companion, but then the check to this growing intimacy had come from myself, and I could not but allow that she had cause for mortification.

At length, turning her face towards me, with the usual cold, demure expression, she said quietly—

"I think you were wrong in expelling young Mr. O'Toole from the boat. It will give great offence."

"Perhaps," I replied, somewhat piqued, "my conduct deprived you of a pleasant companion; if so, I do regret it."

"Your insinuation requires no answer from me," replied she, with composure; "but I do think brawls very undignified.

We have too much of them in this country, and one is the parent of many more. Strangers, particularly, ought to set us a better example."

"My principal reason for so acting towards Mr. Titus O'Toole," said I, reproachfully, "was that I thought his presence near you was an impertinent and unwelcome intrusion."

"Against such persons I can always defend myself. Do not take up the cudgels for me again, Mr. Wyville, I entreat you."

I bowed, but made no reply, resolving in my own mind to take her advice for the future. We were both manifestly little inclined for further conversation, and remained silent till I landed Florence at the Mount, and ordered my men to row me to Rathlynn.

And so ended the pic-nic—like all other pic-nics, productive of little or no pleasure in the retrospect. Mr. Fitzpatrick was angry with his son, and he with his sister. Julia Corrigan returned home peevish and dissatisfied. Titus O'Toole vowed vengeance for the insult he had received, and Mrs. Fitzpatrick declared she had seldom spent so unpleasant a day. As for Florence, she was annoyed at herself and disappointed with me; and as for myself, I felt the proceedings of the day one great mistake, placing me altogether in a wrong position, and promising a future harvest of serious annoyance and discomfort.

Mr. Rosse had been puffing away vigorously at his pipe, as I was reading the latter part of the foregoing chapter. When I ceased he laid it down.

"My dear boy," said he, "take care of yourself. That Irish girl knows what she is about. Egad, she throws her fly, and allures the fish in a very knowing way. Her manner, you observe, is mixed—cloud and sunshine—now intimate and confidential—now distant and reserved. Take care, or she'll gaff you, and then what will the Admiral say, Mr. Frank?"

"You see, sir, I am a little on my guard," said I, not noticing the anachronism.

"What fools men are in the matter of women!" ejaculated Mr. Rosse, as if addressing himself. "It is through our vanity they catch us, Frank. It pleases us right well to think a pretty woman prefers us to all the world besides, and we at once give her credit for good taste and fine feelings. But we do not know, nor are we willing to believe, that the very same game is played again and again with other people till it succeeds. We find all that out afterwards. By all means avoid these pic-nic parties. They are mere matrimonial man-traps. And do not be so ready to flare up when anything goes contrary to your wishes. That girl Florence gave you good advice. A man never looks so like a fool as when he is in a passion—'to be in anger is impiety.' Remember what our great poet says:—

> 'Quarrelling is valour misbegot.
> He's truly valiant that can wisely suffer
> The worst that man can breathe, and make his wrongs
> His outsides, and wear them like his raiment—carelessly,
> And ne'er prefer his injuries to the heart,
> To bring it into danger.'

But, Frank, what is doing on the estate, meanwhile?"

"We shall hear something about that to-morrow, sir."

CHAPTER VIII.

"Hoch man! dear sirs, is that the gate
They waste sae mony a braw estate?"
Burns.

During all this time it must not be supposed that I was idle. I was always an early riser, and herein, agriculturally speaking, lies the secret of progress. I was determined, in spite of their old habits, to have a fair day's work from my labourers in return for a fair day's wages. And this I effected, not by scolding and swearing at them, but by giving them an interest in the work, consulting with them, and hearing their opinions, turning a deaf ear to their slanders of one another (a too common fault among these poor people), and, at the conclusion of any great effort or considerable operation, giving a treat, such as Father Matthew would not complain of, or even sending for the piper, and joining myself heartily in the innocent revel. While with them and among them I had never reason to complain of my Irish labourers. I found them apt, intelligent, lively, good-tempered, and teachable. I wish I could add that when I was away as good a day's work was done as when I was present. It was not so —far from it.

I had taken great pains, by reading and inquiry, to obtain a thorough knowledge of the best methods of dealing with the unpromising tract under my superintendence, and well was it I did so, for in the course of my observations I saw thousands thrown away in so-called improvements, which, from want of judicious management, returned little or no profit on the outlay. Draining, as the foundation and *sine quâ non* of all agricultural success on wet soils, was at first my principal aim, and I endeavoured to improve, at little cost, the surface of the lands, with a view to reletting to advantage.

Reserving, therefore, the tract more immediately about the house for more artistic and expensive treatment, I had, on the very first week of my residence at Rathlynn, collected all the hands I could procure, and dug drains, deep or wide, shallow or narrow, according to the requirements of the soil, till I had removed a great portion of the surface water, and made the soft places sound, and dried up all the plashy pools, which, when I first walked over the estate, had given to it so melancholy and so unpromising an aspect.

No one, but those who have tried it,

could believe the alteration which the judicious application of a little capital will produce in these Hibernian morasses. I was myself perfectly astonished, and when the drains were finished and the cabins re-thatched, and the fences repaired or remade, it looked no longer like the same property.

At the latter end of March, the weather being clear and dry, I set all hands to burning the surface, having skimmed it over with a plough made for the purpose, and it surprised me in what a short space of time I was enabled to cover a large tract with ashes, and plough them in shallowly with selected grass seeds. In the summer the land so treated had changed its brown and barren aspect for one of the brightest verdure. It is true the herbage was at first far from luxuriant, but the changed and changing aspect of the land was most encouraging and pleasing.

Around the house, of course, the most improvement was attempted. The meadows on the margin of the lake were cleared of weeds and stones, and frequently rolled; the old crumbling "ditches" (by which in Ireland is meant "a bank") were thrown down, and replaced by posts and rails, or by young hedges of quickset protected by stake and heather fences. The plantations were also carefully thinned, and much useful wood obtained for the above operations. I had also three strong mules every day bringing up coral sand and sea-weed from the shore, and I purchased all the manure I could lay my hands upon in Mullikeen and the surrounding country.

By commencing all this in time I was enabled to bring a considerable quantity of land into tillage, and my Swedes, and Aberdeens, and mangels, and potatoes, and oats, were the admiration of the neighbourhood.

"Egad," said Mr. Fitzpatrick, one day, as we were walking over the lands, "it's the good example you Saxons set us."

"Then why is it not more universally followed?" I asked with a smile.

"Simply because we want the rhino. That father of yours must have put his hands pretty deep in his pocket, young man, to have kept this sort of thing agoing?"

"My father does not restrict me, but I hope, after all, it will bring more money in than it takes out. If I did not feel assured of this, I should be afraid to act as I do."

"Well, we shall see—I have seldom found improving farmers turn out rich men. Look at old Ned Fogarty; he has never, to my knowledge, laid out one penny on his lands, and I know him to be worth more than five hundred pounds. He stores his money as it comes in; for, as he says, 'If

I laid it out on the land, how much of it should I see again?'"

"He might have quadrupled his five hundred pounds," replied I; "but he is a mere pensioner upon Nature. He just tills enough ground to supply himself with potatoes, and suffers all the rest to remain in its original state of rough pasture."

"True, but he maintains a good dairy, and little that costs him either in manures or labour."

"And yet, some of his land," said I, "properly drained and tilled, would yield him thirty tons of turnips to the acre, and, as they sold last winter at eighteen shillings a ton, you may easily calculate the profit."

"That is as it may be. Ned likes a certainty, like all of us, and we find it easier and surer to stick to the firkin of butter than to waste our gains on horses or mules, or on new-fashioned ploughs and guano."

"Well, for my part," responded I, "I could not sleep to treat land as it is treated here. Everything abstracted, nothing applied. What a different country this would be could only some of our English farmers be persuaded to settle in it. I despair of the natives. Instead of learning, they despise or laugh at improvements; and even the very men who labour on my farm think the whole matter an absurdity. Even you, sir, my neighbour, whose eyes must be open to the substantial benefits of the course I am pursuing, ridicule my efforts and scorn my example. As Horace says, 'Rident vicini glebas et saxa moventum.' I only wish we had a large importation of Saxon farmers among us."

"And why don't they come? There is nothing to hinder them."

"In reality, I do not think there is," I replied—"but the habits of the people here deter them, and there is a general carelessness and untidiness pervading everything, that to their eyes seems beyond cure."

"Then they are right in leaving us to cure ourselves," said Mr. Fitzpatrick. "You may depend upon it, Wyville, that we who are born on the soil best know how to use it."

"To abuse it," rejoined I, mentally; but seeing the subject was not an agreeable one I remained silent.

Nothing, indeed will teach some of these Irish gentlemen *—they know little or nothing, but are quite satisfied with that little, and look upon improvers as a species of contemptible enthusiasts. Few of them farm much themselves, and they prefer squeezing out of their tenants the utmost farthing they can get, thinking that all their duties as landlords are comprised in

* I am speaking of fifteen years ago.

"receiving rent!" They can walk their lands in pursuit of game, but they care not to see them without gates, without fences, choked with weeds, poisoned with rushes, a melancholy and disgusting scene of sloth and squalid wretchedness. That there are exceptions I am most willing to allow, and the operation of that most invaluable boon to Ireland, "the Encumbered Estates Court," has been the means, in many cases, of breaking up large mismanaged properties, and introducing a better race of proprietors, more willing to be taught, and more eager to improve what they have thus acquired. As I told my father in one of my letters,—"I never saw so grateful a soil, or one on which a judicious outlay would so soon repay itself." In his usual laconic way, he replied in his next letter—"I believe what you say, and you have liberty to draw upon me for what you require."

But my most successful effort was in two large patches of land which adjoined Rathlynn, terminating on the east, at the dingle I have before noticed as being on the way to "the Mount." This belonged to Mr. Fitzpatrick, but he kindly relinquished it to the Admiral for a very handsome sum, one-third of which was paid into the hands of his solicitor, Mr. O'Folio, of Mullikeen, on the understanding that an abstract of title should be furnished in a short time, and the matter finally settled. I did not write to my father on the subject till I had received both from Mr. Fitzpatrick and his attorney a very decided and ready assurance that the title was unexceptionable. Of this there could be but little doubt indeed, as the property had descended to the present possessor through three generations at least. These fields skirted the lake, and being in a particularly conspicuous situation, I had bestowed more than usual pains and expense upon them, anxious to show my neighbours what could be done. And certainly my crops there of mangels and Swedes could not be surpassed in the district. I had thoroughly underdrained the land, cleaned, fenced, and manured it well, and, as usual, quadrupled its former value.

Often would Mr. Fitzpatrick, accompanied by his daughter Florence, join me there, and watch my operations with interest; the father smiling dubiously, if not contemptuously—the daughter, with more good sense and feeling, signifying her hearty approval.

"I have no doubt," she would say, "that if you remain here you will be amply repaid in pocket, but if you fancy that you will obtain disciples I fear you will be mistaken. A century will not make Ireland industrious. No prejudices so cling to a man as those that contribute to his ease. My countrymen would like the result, but think it inadequate to the labour."

And sometimes, when her father went away, Florence would still linger; she would sit on a rock with her book—she would bring me a flower and inquire its name—or she would stroll along the margin of the Lough, where I sometimes (not always) joined her, and perhaps escorted her home, and there spent the evening.

Towards me, indeed, her manner was become more friendly; she loved to talk of England—to inquire after the tastes, pursuits and habits of our ladies; she would know the condition of our peasantry—our farmers and our tradespeople—the state of our towns and cities—and she often beguiled me into talking of my own family, of my father, my sister, and of my uncle Rosse, and the life I had led under his hospitable roof.

To one isolated like myself all this was very pleasant, and I thought it very harmless, and began to feel disappointed if a few days were to pass away and I did not see my fair friend. Yet I was not in love—nor did she disturb my dreams. It was a pleasant *divertissement* in my somewhat monotonous mode of life, and as I kept clear of all dangerous subjects when we were together, I did not feel that, by even the most precise, my conduct could be called in question. My engagement to my father was vividly before me, and made me cautious, and, with *Luciana* in the comedy, my resolution was—

"Ere I learn love, I'll practise to obey."

CHAPTER IX.

> "But how can I to that lady ride
> With saving of my dignitie?
> Oh! a curch and mantle ye may wear,
> And in my cloak ye shall muffled be."
>
> *Christie's Will.*

AUTUMN was now coming to a conclusion, and though the weather still continued fine and open, yet we every day expected a change. The business of the farm was nearly completed—the ricks were made and thatched, the potatoes and mangels stored, and the Swedes thrown into small heaps in the field, and covered up with mould. I looked with pleasure upon the generally successful result of my various operations, and on comparing the cost with the marketable value of my stock, live and dead, I felt that the Admiral would have no cause for dissatisfaction. Besides, the improvement in the surface of the property was, for the time, almost incredible. It is astonishing, as I have already observed, how small an outlay will totally alter the aspect of many of these Irish estates; and money, judiciously expended, will yield a large return, even in the way of rent. An Irish farmer will pay most liberally for those improvements he never even dreamed of executing himself.

As I now felt at leisure, I determined to have a full fling of recreation, and accordingly I summoned Larry Lanigan, and ordering him to prepare the boat and be in readiness, walked down to "the Mount;" perchance Archibald would accompany me. I met Florence half way; she was standing on the wooden bridge in the Dingle. She informed me that her brother was gone to Mullikeen to spend the day with the Corrigans, and would not return till night. Her face was flushed, and her manner had an assumed calmness that manifestly was intended to hide some intensity of feeling.

Finding my position somewhat awkward, I was retreating, when she motioned me to stay, and after a short pause, she inquired in a careless tone whether this "was one of my busy days?"

I replied, "Certainly not. I was intending to spend the day on the mountains."

"Then you cross the lake in the boat?"

I said that was my intention.

"Would you, then, do me a favour, Mr. Wyville?" said she, in a tone of some agitation. "Will you land me under the rocks in the Middle Lake, and call for me there as you return?"

I hesitated.

"You need not fear," rejoined she, significantly; "my father and mother are also at Mullikeen, and no notice can be taken of my absence. If you knew how much was involved in this trifling request, you would not refuse me."

"I would refuse you nothing, Miss Florence," said I, in great perplexity, "which I ought to grant, but——"

"I should not ask *you*, had I any other means of accomplishing my object. It pains me to draw so largely on your benevolence, and I am conscious that I hazard your good opinion in the course I am adopting—but I have no alternative, and have weighed the matter well before I ventured to act."

I still hesitated, when, with all a woman's quickness who has a point to gain, she said,—

"Thank you, then, a thousand times—

we will not loiter here—I will take the path to the waterfall—meet me there—no one can observe us when you are once round the little promontory."

She hurried off, leaving me in a fit of amazement, and I stood motionless, looking after her as she disappeared through the thick bushes.

Deliberation was now vain. I could not suffer her to walk to the spot indicated and fail to meet her there. Such an act I felt would degrade her in her own eyes, nay, be a positive insult. And, perhaps, after all, it was a kind action, and even if observed could be explained by her so as not in any way to compromise me. Comforting myself as well as I could with this assurance, I hailed the boat, and to my further surprise found no one was in her but a little boy of Larry's, who informed me that his father was gone to fetch the cross line, and would meet me at Flynn's cottage, on the Upper Lake, where he supposed I should be going. Having said this, the urchin bolted off, saying he must "go and tell his father that my honour was just starting."

Walking slowly up to the house I got my gun, and loosed the dogs, and was soon rowing vigorously to the appointed spot. It was still early, and it would be three hours yet ere the sun would attain his meridian. It was one of those beautiful autumnal days, so bright and clear, so temperate and enjoyable; I was in high spirits, and anticipated a delightful ramble over the mountains. Some grouse there were, and golden plover in abundance, and possibly the woodcocks might have sent over a forward flight, as the last few nights had been frosty, with occasional fog from the sea, and after all, landing Florence at Craigddhu, and even bringing her back again in the evening, would be no great interruption to my day's sport. And how considerate it was of her to walk to the waterfall, a spot where we were not at all likely to be observed. But how was it that Larry had not obeyed my summons? Would it not have been better to have had him in the boat? Yes—no—certainly there were *pros* and *cons*—he might chatter, and wink, and nod as was his custom. After all, perhaps, it was more prudent to go alone,—and yet—but it was no use thinking—the thing must be done—but I would take care another time that I would steer clear of such a dilemma, cost what it would.

Of such a nature were my reflections as I urged my light boat along the calm surface of the Lough. Rounding the little promontory, I ran into shallow water, just where a mountain stream threw itself into the lake, and leaping on shore I chained the boat to the boll of a silver birch whose graceful boughs kissed the waters as they rippled past.

It was a sweet, secluded spot where I stood. A stream, having its source in a small lake high up in the mountain, came foaming and dashing down its side; now throwing itself in airy cascades over ledges of rock—now boiling in deeply-worn cavities, or gliding more smoothly where gentler slopes arrested its more rapid progress. Birches and alders, and tufted ferns, and heaths of curious variety, fringed the margin of this crystal brook, and it was pleasant to track its progress from above, and to pause in delighted contemplation of its deep pools and tiny cataracts.

On gaining the land I looked around, but no one appeared, and following the path a short distance up the stream, I sat down on a grey rock which overhung a clear deep pool, into which the foaming waters of the rivulet threw themselves over a ledge of rock about fifteen feet above. It was a lovely sequestered spot, and one I had often visited in my excursions on the Lough.

It was not long ere I was joined by my companion. Her air was grave and melancholy, and without further greeting she took her seat at my side.

"I have a thousand apologies to make for the liberty I have taken," said she, casting her eyes downwards; "and I feel that what I have done does not bear reflection. But the welfare not only of my brother but of the whole family is at stake, and I have been quite bewildered how to act. Had I employed any other means of effecting my purpose, I should have been discovered; I therefore resolved to throw myself on your friendship. I believe I *may* count you as a friend. Mr Wyville?"

"Most certainly," I replied, rising to break up a somewhat dangerous conference.

"One moment more and we will go," said she, placing her hand on my arm. "I feel it due to you—and to myself also—to give you some explanation of the step I have taken. I have told you that my brother is engaged to Julia Corrigan. She is much attached to him, and in the peculiar relation that exists between the two families, the consummation of this engagement is not only desirable, but is absolutely necessary for the future welfare of our family. How or why I need not say; perhaps your own sagacity will point it out. But this new connection Archibald is forming, will be positive ruin. I alone have discovered it, and I, too, must prevent it, if possible. And yet I cannot do this unaided. And who is there I can trust? Not one—and, therefore, my only alternative is to make a friend, even though in so doing I transgress, or appear to do so, the usual laws that bind down and tie our sex. Oh, Mr. Wyville! you do not know how severely I feel all this! The whole affair is so contrary to my nature and my habits! Yet I have carefully weighed matters, and I see no other plan than to claim your good offices, though at the same time I feel, I know, that I am forfeiting your good opinion. I know I can trust you — you are an Englishman — manly, honourable, and fearless. I must and will break off this connection — and you will assist me?" She clung to my arm, and looked up into my face with those fine eyes full of entreaty and confidence, adding, with peculiar emphasis,—

"I know you will!"

I did not answer, but took her arm

within mine, for the ground was rough, and we walked on silently together.

In what a pretty net was I entangling myself! And yet, what could I do? To repulse a lady in distress, and one, too, like Florence Fitzpatrick, I would not. Things must take their course, and I must act as prudently as possible under the peculiar circumstances in which I was placed.

We gained the boat, and I rowed quickly along the shore, keeping as much as possible the shelter of the woods. I observed that my companion had thrown on a summer cloak of her father's, which, falling from her head downwards, effectually concealed her person. This reassured me. I ventured to inquire what was her present purpose.

"To see the young woman," said she, "to tell her that my brother is engaged, and to warn her of the danger she is incurring in forming any connection with him."

"Have you seen this person, then?"

"No—when I attempted it on the day we went up the Lough, I was miserably foiled, and glad to escape, even, without injury. There is a mystery about those people I cannot solve—but you may."

"How?"

"I will tell you everything, can I only make sure of your co-operation."

I was silent, and shook my head.

"Then you will not help me?"

"I dare not, must not interfere in what does not concern me. Only reflect for one moment, Miss Fitzpatrick, what might be the consequences of my unauthorized meddling."

"Do not be so ceremonious, Mr. Wyville," said she, smiling through her tears, "as to call me Miss Fitzpatrick. You have promised me your friendship, and friends may well drop such an affix as 'Miss.' Call me Florence. As to consequences, you need not fear. I guard *you* more anxiously than I do myself, and I am quite prepared for any *contretemps* that may arise. You may trust a woman's foresight and prudence in such matters as these. We will not betray one another."

I could not mistake the feelings which at this moment threw my fair companion off her guard, and I could easily foresee the reward that would be mine if I made the most of the present opportunity. The love of Florence I felt was within my reach, would I only participate in her plans; and truly, as I looked upon that fine form and countenance, I was strangely tempted to yield to the delusion. But my promise to my father, like the opposing angel, stopped me in the way, and I sat silent, urging the boat along with all my might.

I have often wondered since at my own resolution. There is nothing so dangerous as a woman's tenderness and a woman's confidence. Thousands fall into this net, and mistake temporary excitement for love. I might have done so too, but I had been early taught "to obey."

I landed my fair charge at the spot she indicated—the cottage of one Flynn, a small mountain farmer, about half a mile below Ballybog, and leaving my boat in a retired cove at no great distance, I loosed my dogs, and slowly ascended the precipitous ranges before me.

CHAPTER X.

"The love that follows us sometimes is our trouble."
Macbeth.

I HAD a glorious day. Bagged four brace and a half of grouse, and two of the blue mountain hare, which, considering the ground was not preserved, and subject to be overrun by every species of vermin, from a shepherd's dog to a marten cat, was pretty well. At least, I was well satisfied, and so was Larry Lanigan, who, hearing the report of my gun, had joined me early in the day.

On questioning him, I could get no satisfactory account of why he did not meet me in the boat. Pat does not generally like being questioned.

"Sure then it *was* I that did that same, and why not?"

"Why not, do you say? Simply because I sent for you to come to me, and I said nothing about the cross line. What reason had you for looking after that, instead of attending the boat?"

"What raison, master? Sure I have always a raison, though I do not always know what it is myself."

"But on this occasion, Larry, perhaps you *can* tell me?"

"Have it all your own way, master, for what's the use of me argyfying the matter with a gentleman of your larning? Gondoutha! I have not another word to say about it."

The sun was already declining in the

heavens, when I thought it full time to return to Flynn's cottage, where I was again to meet Florence Fitzpatrick. After a quick walk of about two miles, we gained a spot where a path diverged two ways—the one towards the foot of the Lough, and the other apparently to the head. Sending Larry on to Rathlynn by the former, and committing to his charge the dogs, the gun, and game-bag, I at once pursued the latter, making sure that it would bring me out at Flynn's cottage.

I had walked briskly for a mile and more, when I found myself on the edge of a wild valley. Below were half enclosed, rough pastures, in which several cows, of the diminutive country sort, were quietly grazing. Blocking up this vale on my left, was a ridge stretching quite across it, and the chimneys of some inhabited house, as I judged by the smoke, peeped out from a straggling grove that crowned that portion of the eminence. Beyond I caught a glimpse of the lake and the distant Glenlara mountains.

Where could I be? It was manifest that I had lost my way, but how to regain it was now the question. The evening would soon draw in, and Florence would be impatient. There was nothing for it but to make my way to the dwelling before me, and seek for directions there.

The foot-path led across the valley, and took a direction too much to the right, so that I was obliged to force my way through a tangled thicket of underwood, so intermixed with brambles and briers that my face, hands, and clothes soon began to experience their effects. Scarcely had I made my way through these impediments, than another, of a yet more formidable character, presented itself. The land at the foot of the ridge on which the house stood was turbary, and had been cut away in broad, deep dykes, so as almost to bar any access to the dwelling, at least on this side. Whether this was the intention, or merely to drain the bog, I could not tell. Be that as it may, the obstacle was serious.

I stood for some time musing what was the best course. To descend into the dyke and then to climb up the other side was hazardous, for when at the bottom of the dyke, so great was the depth, that the probability was I should not be able to get out again on either side.

In this dilemma I looked round with anxiety and alarm—the evening would soon close in, and it might be dark by the time I reached Flynn's cottage. I was turning away to seek some other exit from this valley of horrors—for, indeed, it looked gloomy, wild, and dank—when my eye glanced accidentally on an old building close down by the bog, the sides of which had been boarded with slabs of timber, and the roof thatched with rushes. A thought at once struck me. A few of these slabs might bridge over the dyke in its narrowest part, and I could thus get clear of my difficulties.

The execution soon followed the thought —the dyke did not exceed seven feet in its narrowest width, and the slabs I had detached were nearly ten feet, so that by fixing them on a large tuft of rushes on either side, I at last found myself safe on terra-firma. Any attempt to leap the dyke would have resulted in a fall probably into it, as the sides were soft and slippery.

Looking around, as I did not see any human being, I stole quietly through the tall grove of trees, in order to reconnoitre; and gaining the summit of the ridge, I found, with astonishment, that the Upper Lake was before me, and that in all probability the house I had arrived at was no other than Ballybog!

The position of this mysterious spot was quite in accordance with its character. I never saw a wilder or a more secluded place. The ridge on which it stood stretched along till lost in higher ground; and it commanded on the west the dark, inhospitable valley I had passed through, and on the east it was only separated from the Lough by a green but suspicious-looking bog. It was very manifest that the inmates of this strange dwelling were not very sociably inclined, for there were no facilities of approach, visible at least, whereas the impediments were numerous and formidable.

As my eye quickly discerned these facts, I must confess to some uneasiness, and I could not help surmising that my escape from this spell-bound ridge would be as difficult on the one side as the approach had been on the other. Summoning courage, however, I made a long and cautious circuit of the house, hoping to meet with some living creature to speak to; but, no—not a sound invaded the universal silence.

I am no coward, but certainly the aspect of things did by no means reassure me. I now remembered how pale and agitated Florence Fitzpatrick was when she returned from her fruitless visit to the same spot; and everything around so decidedly convinced me that my presence there was an intrusion, that my only anxiety now was to get clear of the place as quickly and as quietly as I could.

I recollected the path that led to the margin of the lake, and determined to gain it if possible. Forcing my way through tangled brakes and uneven ground, I at length emerged upon a kind of lawn or open space, where the house stood revealed before me, and there, standing in a kind of rude porch, was a young female, and a huge dog watchfully crouching at her feet.

My first impulse was to advance, cap in hand—but I paused a moment to observe. The girl was fair and beautiful I saw at a glance. Her head, according to the fashion of the country, was partly covered with the Spanish mantilla, and, though not too tall, her size was good, and her figure full and graceful.

But to observe this was the work of a moment, for another matter now engaged all my attention—no less than to take care of myself. The girl uttered a faint exclamation of surprise as I was about to advance, and, without one moment's hesitation, set the huge brute upon me. I had no weapon of defence, not even a stick, and I saw at once that my only chance was in flight—for there was still a considerable distance between me and my antagonist. In an instant I darted across the lawn, casting a by no means amiable glance at my fair persecutor, and, finding an open space in the wood beyond, I pursued it for some distance, the dog gaining rapidly upon me, when suddenly my course was impeded by a high turf-bank, manifestly intended as the boundary of the domain. To win this, then, would place me in safety. I did not hesitate, but with one bound cleared the fence, and found myself on the other side—secure, indeed, but knee-deep in a quagmire!

The sun had just sunk behind the distant mountains when, annoyed and angry, I reached Flynn's cottage, and there found Florence waiting impatiently for my arrival.

"It is an hour beyond the time you appointed," said she, rather reproachfully—I fear we shall not reach the waterfall before the night closes in. But what is the matter, Mr. Wyville?" continued she, eyeing first my face and then my soiled dress—"have you been contending with the wild cattle of the hills, or had a tussle with the 'good people?'"

"I lost my way," replied I, "and in my anxiety not to keep you waiting, braved both bog and brake to join you at the time proposed. But it was all of no use, and I am glad, indeed, to find myself here at all."

"I hope you are not hurt," said she, in a tone of alarm; "that would, indeed, mark this day as doubly unfortunate."

"How so?" replied I, not able to conjecture what she meant. "Have you, too, had some misadventure?"

"I will tell you when we are in the

boat. Here every tree and bush is a spy."

Right stoutly did I row when we were once more upon the Lough. I felt the danger of arriving late at "the Mount," and our light skiff shot along the smooth waters, leaving a long track behind. I was too much occupied to talk, and Florence remained silent, wrapped in her cloak, and seemingly too much absorbed in her own thoughts to address any words to me.

Twilight was fading into gloom when we reached the waterfall. I handed my companion out of the boat, and she hastily bade me good night, and was hurrying up the path in the direction of "the Mount," when I entreated her to wait one moment. She half paused, and I quickly fastened the boat to a tree and joined her.

"You shall not go alone, Miss Florence —I must see you safe home."

"By no means," replied she; "*Miss*

Florence" (emphatically) "is too much accustomed to tread these wilds alone, to need any escort."

"But I think, for several reasons, I had better walk home than cross the lake. We can part where the path divides, and you will then be within a few yards of your own domain."

"Perhaps you are right," said she; "we shall escape notice, if no one sees you passing our house to Rathlynn."

I took her arm, and we walked gently on. It was a fresh and balmy evening, and the stars began already to twinkle above our heads. We both felt how much the events of the day had torn down the barriers of reserve, and how rapidly our mutual sympathies were increasing.

Florence Fitzpatrick was, indeed, a fine, intellectual, lovable woman, and one whose notice and regard were not to be easily or generally obtained. I acknowledged all this as we walked on side by side, in a silence more dangerous than words. At length I felt bound to speak, and I inquired whether her expedition had succeeded?

"No better than the last," replied she, in some agitation; "and what is to be done now, I know not. I must and will extinguish this foolish and dangerous flirtation, if, indeed, it is nothing more."

"Then you could not obtain an interview?"

"No; I met instead with a rude repulse. Paradise itself was not better guarded—yet the place looks gloomy and dreary as a place of torment. It is well named Ballybog. If I was not a female, I would soon unravel this mystery. But what can I do more than has been done? I feel as if I had already hazarded too much."

Her dark eyes were fixed upon me for

an instant, and I felt her arm tremble in mine.

"Yes, indeed, success could be my only excuse for such unusual conduct as mine; but did you know all, you would not blame me, Mr. Wyville. You are manly and humane, and will make every allowance—some day, perhaps, you will know more."

"Can I be of further use to you?" said I, compassionating the painful state of her feelings. "If I can, without injury to either of us, promote your wishes, I am ready to do so. Shall I see the girl herself?"

"Oh, no!" replied she, hastily, "I do not wish that!—your interference there would do no good — but the contrary. No, no, you cannot assist me *there*, therefore do not attempt it. You might, perhaps, influence my brother. Let him understand he is watched. You need not tell him the cause—but merely say that you have reason to know that it is so. Surely that alone would alarm him. But your attempting to obtain access at Ballybog would be worse than useless. It would involve us all in a skein we might never unravel. But here the path divides. Good night."

CHAPTER XI.

"Our feasts in every mess have folly."
Winter's Tale.

On reaching Rathlynn, which I did without meeting any one, I found Nelly Sweeny on the look-out for me. Nelly was a bright-eyed, smart Irish girl, assistant and maid-of-all-work to my housekeeper, Mrs. Doran, who was herself a slim, tall, and somewhat pompous lady, with a huge bundle of complimentary "discharges"* from various families in and near the good old Protestant town of Derry. With the exception

* Characters from former employers.

of Larry's occasional services, they formed the whole of my present establishment.

As I turned the corner of the house, there was Nelly, with her two hands up to her eyes, gazing earnestly up the lake, and screaming out at the top of her voice to Mrs. Doran in the kitchen.

"Bad 'cess to me, ma'am, it is not the master I can see, at all, at all, nor yet the boat; if I'd look my eyes out I will see nothing but the black hills, and the dark waters, and the little stars up there just winking at us. Sure it's time he should be snug at home."

"And so I am snug at home, Nelly," said I, "and go in and tell Mrs. Doran to cook me something, for I've had more work than feasting since I left Rathlynn."

"Bannaght Dheah!" exclaimed Nelly, turning round suddenly; "the master's come—the master's come!" she cried out, running to the kitchen window; "and musha, ma'am, he's had nothing to eat this blessed day."

"Then go in, my gra gal," said I, "and tell Mrs. Doran to make haste."

Nelly vanished, and I sank down on a rustic seat which in the day-time commanded a grand and imposing view of the lake and mountains. Now all was dark, except that a few stars twinkled over head, and the gloomy outline of the mountains was faintly visible against the sky. No sound was heard, but a gentle murmur from the waters of the lake breaking quietly on the shore below. The excitement of the day was passed, and my thoughts rambled over the strange events that had occurred.

Though I really was not much to blame as far as Florence was concerned, yet I felt my conduct was liable to misconstruction.

What would be thought by her family if they were acquainted with the events of the past day? And was it right or prudent to do anything which they ought not to know? And what might be the result of our joint intermeddling in the concerns of the younger Fitzpatrick? Would he not have good reason to complain? And, moreover, my review of Archibald's character did not reassure me. I knew him to be bold and unscrupulous, impatient of control, and reckless of consequences. As fellow-sportsmen we had always agreed well together, but any collision with him, I well knew, was better avoided.

Yet I could not resist a feeling of extraordinary interest in the recluse family at Ballybog, and I longed to ascertain who they were, and how far and for what real purpose Archibald had accomplished an acquaintance with them. And yet, after all, what had I to do with the matter? What was this mysterious family to me? And why should I continue a kind of confidential intercourse with Mr. Fitzpatrick's daughter, which might have the most perplexing results?

Clearly at that moment did I see my position, and well were it if, on all occasions of excitement, time was but given for the calm exercise of our reason. I resolved upon double caution, to see less of my neighbours at "the Mount," and to turn my entire attention to the improvement of the estate.

With this determination I rose and hastened to partake of the salmon cutlets and mutton steak which my good housekeeper had hastily prepared for my refection. I found that during my absence Mr. D'Arcie had called upon me, and he had left a note of invitation to spend the day at Doonore on the ensuing Thursday. I was glad of this opportunity of being seen elsewhere than at the Fitzpatricks', and readily undertook to appear.

On the day appointed I started early, and the two boys, Mick and Dan, rowed me to the Upper Lake. I had a change of dress, my gun, and an active spaniel, and was fortunate enough to bag two couples of woodcocks, being, as I knew, the earliest that had been shot that season. These, I knew, would prove a most acceptable present to Colonel D'Arcie, who never carried a gun, owing to some wound that still disabled his right arm.

The family at Doonore were agreeable, well-bred people, lively and happy in their solitude, and much attached to each other. Mrs. D'Arcie was an English lady, and as Mr. D'Arcie had entered the army early, and served abroad for many years in an

English regiment, there was scarcely the slightest tinge of Irishism either in their habits or their speech. Indeed Mrs. D'Arcie had a perfect horror of the brogue, and as it was determined, when the girls were old enough to be formally introduced, to remove to England for a few years, they did not care being on very familiar terms with their neighbours. They kept up, indeed, a proper social feeling, but it was not a house where parties were admitted indiscriminately at all times and all hours.

Though so often passing close to Doonore in our various fishing excursions, neither Archibald nor I ever called without invitation; indeed I often thought the Fitzpatricks were no particular favourites, and I knew the O'Tooles were considered vulgar. However, when once there, visitors were assured of a hearty welcome, and in the somewhat stately civility of Colonel D'Arcie, the well-bred affability of his lady, and the lively unaffected manners of the junior members of the family, every one felt happy and at ease.

I had lately, since the pic-nic, been several times at Doonore, and found myself a special object of regard to the boys as having been at an English University, and as being a tolerable sportsman, while the girls almost monopolized one at the piano, where I could take a second to their songs, or accompany them in a glee.

"I think Mr. Wyville is very well for an Englishman, Fanny, don't you?" said Susan, one evening, after we had closed the piano.

"For an Englishman?" said I; "Why *for* an Englishman?"

"Because, you know, Englishmen are generally very proud and stupid, and you are not so *very*."

"Thank you for the compliment, I feel it. And so I am just a little less proud and stupid than most of my countrymen?"

"Yes, don't you think so, Fanny?"

"I almost fancy I do," replied Miss Fanny, laughing heartily.

"Of course," said I, "you know a great deal about the English, Miss Susan?"

"I ought to do — mamma is from England."

"And if Mrs. D'Arcie had been born on the Don or the Volga, you would, by the same rule, be perfectly acquainted with the Cossacks and Calmuc Tartars."

"Oh, Mr. Wyville, I never thought of such a thing. I'll tell mamma, I declare, what you say of her. But, at any rate, we all agree that if you continue to improve, you will, in time, be almost as lively, and as pleasant, and as little conceited as—who shall I say?—as Mr. Titus O'Toole!"

It was scarcely noon when I moored my boat at the landing-place at Doonore, and on entering the house I was told the family were in the grounds. I was surprised, on joining them, to find a large party. The Fitzpatricks, the O'Tooles, and the Corrigans, and a tall, respectable-looking ecclesiastic, who was introduced to me as Father Roche.

Preparations were making for an archery meeting; the butts were up—the ground measured—the grass mown. All were in the highest spirits, and after a luncheon *al fresco* the sport was to commence.

The O'Flesks and other parties began to pour in, and Colonel D'Arcie stalked about as if he was at the head of his regiment, giving orders and promulgating regulations. As the day was fine, and even warm, a table loaded with refreshments was spread under the shade of a magnificent beech, and we all sat down to eat, drink, and be merry. As each gentleman was to select a lady, I approached Susan D'Arcie, but she shook her head saucily, and said she was engaged to Mr. Titus O'Toole.

"Only think," said she, in a whisper, "Florence has declined his companionship, and so he has fixed upon me, for which I do not thank him. I suppose," added she, archly, "that Florence expects *you?*"

"I don't suppose anything of the kind," replied I, hastily. "Is your sister, Miss Fanny, engaged? I don't see her."

"Yes, there she is with Mr. Tom Daly. You *must* take Florence out, Mr. Wyville. I am sure she expects you."

The little lively mischief-maker laughed heartily, and left me somewhat discomposed. I dreaded the slightest suspicion of anything existing between Florence and myself, beyond mere common acquaintanceship, and I could not help feeling both vexed and annoyed at Susan D'Arcie's insinuation.

I felt also that, for the future, great caution was necessary on my side.

As I was standing irresolute, Colonel D'Arcie approached, and taking my arm, led me up to Florence.

"I need not introduce such near neighbours, Mr. Wyville—will you take out Miss Fitzpatrick?"

I was not displeased, and yet I felt all the blood in my body mount into my cheeks, and beat in my heart. I was about to offer my arm, when Florence said calmly,—

"I am engaged to Mr. Gorman O'Flesk."

Mr. D'Arcie seemed surprised, but quickly added,—

"Well then, Mr. Wyville, you must look out for yourself—by-the-bye, I see Mary Daly is disengaged—she is a nice girl—here, Mary, I bring you an English partner, I hope you will be kind to him, my dear."

This little episode brought me immense relief, and I now hoped the perplexities of the day were over. But it did not so prove.

It was arranged at the archery that each gentleman should score with his partner, and there was, accordingly, a double prize. My partner was a pretty, quiet, and rather winning little girl of seventeen—having few new ideas, but pleased to be talked to, and with a ready laugh that was not discouraging.

It cannot be supposed that there was much good shooting among the Glenlara mountains. The ladies certainly had the best of it, and towards the conclusion, Florence and her partner, who was an awkward young man, and a bad shot, had scored equal to Miss Daly and myself. In fact, it was manifest that the contest now lay between Florence and me. I had resolved in my own mind how it should terminate, when I overheard Fanny D'Arcie say to young Daly,—

"I am sorry for poor Mary, for Mr. Wyville will never think of carrying off the prize from Florence; mark if he does."

This turned the scale—I won the prize, and had the pain (it was indeed no pleasure) of presenting a handsome brooch, in the form of an Irish harp, to my pretty partner, and of appropriating to myself a drinking-horn of ancient pattern, surmounted with silver.

I was angry at my own sensations. I felt as if I had robbed Florence of what was justly her due, for my partner was a much better shot than hers—he, indeed, never made a hit. It would have delighted me if she had obtained the prize—but I feared to forego any advantage, lest remarks might be made. She bore it well, however, and had the tact to act towards me, during the whole day, with a manner so natural and unembarrassed as was calculated to foil the keenest observers.

To wind up the festivities by daylight, a boat-race was proposed, and this was won by half a length by Archibald Fitzpatrick, who received as his prize a pair of oars, sent for expressly from Belfast.

As the evening began to close, we retired into the house, and sat down to a plentiful repast, all in the highest apparent good-humour. Partners were changed, and even a dance was hinted at. Colonel D'Arcie again took me up to Miss Fitzpatrick.

"The two best archers should certainly take the top of the table."

"Then Mary Daly is entitled to that honour," said Florence; "she wears the prize."

"You scored four times as much as poor

Mary," said the Colonel. "That is all nonsense. Do as I tell you, Florence. I think Mr. Wyville ought to be offended."

"I am already engaged to Mr. Titus O'Toole."

"Indeed! then I have nothing further to say," replied Colonel D'Arcie, looking archly at me.

I could not help admiring the self-possession and tact she displayed; it again reassured me, and I felt, at any rate, quite secure in the prudence and foresight of my late *compagnon de voyage.* Her joining herself to the stiff, pragmatical Mr. Titus was a masterpiece of policy; at the same time, I well knew it was gall and wormwood to her.

My neighbour at dinner was Fanny D'Arcie, a lively, agreeable girl, not handsome—and on the other side of the table was her sister Susan, bantering merrily with Archibald Fitzpatrick. There had been a slight pause in the boisterous mirth of the party when Susan called to me across the table—

"By-the-bye, Mr. Wyville, you passed Doonore a few days ago in your boat, and, though we shouted and waved our handkerchiefs, you did not condescend to take any notice."

"Because," replied I, "of course I did not see you."

"You must have been very much absorbed, then. Who was the person that sat at the stern? He seemed muffled up as if he had a face-ache."

I will not describe what I felt at this moment, nor do I know how I should have got out of the dilemma, had not Larry, who had been detained to assist in waiting, upset a dish of smoking hot potatoes into Mr. Fitzpatrick's lap—a feat which that gentleman resented as an Irish gentleman ought to do. Great was the uproar—Larry apologising, his victim threatening, becalling, and abusing, till the gentleman in the boat with the face-ache seemed entirely forgotten, and I once more resumed my serenity.

Never can I forget the quick glance which Florence threw across at me as Susan D'Arcie was speaking. It told me to be bold and self-possessed as she was. But how infinitely do women on such occasions surpass us in that latter quality! It was manifest her whole conduct had been regulated with a view to disarm suspicion, and to set at rest a surmise that the young Englishman was more than usually attentive to the daughter of his next neighbour. In this I could see nothing but magnanimity, and if, by a concurrence of circumstances, she had forced me into a false position, she proved that she was by no means disposed to take advantage of it.

Yet all these strange events began to have a manifest influence on my own mind. They promoted a secret sympathy between Florence and myself. We felt, when thrown together, a more than common bond of intimacy, and when absent we perfectly understood that we thought of each other. And yet not the slightest allusion had ever been made to any feeling warmer than friendship, nor, in fact, did such really exist on my side. What might have arisen I will not say—but my father's injunction acted as a perpetual check, and caused me to be more cautious than is natural to a young man who well knows that one step in advance would make the prize his own.

But much as I admired Florence as a fine, sensible, and independent young woman, and one who stood out superior to the circle in which she was placed, yet I did not equally admire her family. Mr. Fitzpatrick was too "easy" to be very agreeable to me, and Archibald, though a pleasant dashing companion in a day's sport, was at best an idle, ignorant squireen, tyrannical and haughty in his manners, and somewhat licentious in his conversation and habits. Between him and me, I know not why, there had of late sprung up a degree of coolness; we went out seldom together, and he had ceased to give me his confidence. Did he think I was intermeddling in his projects at Ballybog?

It was past midnight when the party broke up. The Fitzpatricks returned home in their car, and my two boys and Larry attended with the boat. Father Roche begged me to land him at a place called the Castle Point, and as there was a bright moon he said he would prefer to walk the remainder of the distance to his house.

The Priest was an agreeable man, more tutored in the ways of the world than is usual with his order, and he had a mild and gentlemanly bearing which was pleasing and attractive. I am sure *he* did not think in his heart that every Protestant would be handed over to perdition. Indeed I myself had observed that his charities and good offices were undiscriminating, and regarded neither race nor creed. As our own clergyman, a young zealot from Dublin, never looked after his own poor, but misspent all his time in "abuse" of the Papists, in order to promote what he termed their "conversion," I had sent my donation for parochial purposes to Father Roche, as I well knew it would be properly and impartially distributed, not wishing, indeed, that it should be appropriated to the purchase of trashy tracts, or lavished in the maintenance of a so-called Scripture-reader. Prejudice and error are not to be overcome by violence or insult, and the conversion of Irish Papists must be, under Providence, their own spontaneous act. Scripture-readers and Protestant missionaries will never effect it.

As we sat side by side at the stern of the boat (Larry was at the bow smoking his dudeen tranquilly), we could converse freely without risk of being overheard.

"Do you like Ireland?" questioned the priest somewhat abruptly.

"Yes; but it will be a more desirable country for residence some fifty years hence."

"When emigration has left it to be peopled by Saxons, I suppose."

"I did not mean that quite. I should rather say when the Saxon and Celtic elements are so blended as to give a new impulse to the population. Ireland is essentially an undeveloped country?"

"It is; but the increased facilities of communication between the two islands will of themselves effect a great change. And yet I do not deny that our people are sadly deficient in enterprise and energy."

"Will self-interest ever teach them?" said I.

"It may by-and-by, and I do hope to see the day when a Celt will be ashamed of his mud cabin, his scantily-stocked garden, and the pestilential dung-heap before his door. While these sights disgrace the country, there is no hope. Dirt and ignorance ever dwell under the same roof."

"I am surprised, sir," said I, "to hear such sentiments from you. The Roman Catholic clergy have been often blamed for not interfering to prevent such a state of things."

"I know they have, and most unjustly. But, sir, the Catholic clergy are not, as a body, quite so bad as the English would believe them to be. The many suffer for the sins of the few. There are many among us who would raise the moral habits of the people, who would rejoice to see them loyal, industrious, and educated. There are some, I confess, and they are the most prominent generally, who care for none of these things, but reduce our sublime faith into a mere political engine. We have mentioned the squalid habits of the people. The clergy are not responsible altogether for that. My own case is one in point. You know my feeling on the subject, but what can I do? I have no funds to build better dwellings, and I have no influence with the landlord, who is a Protestant, as is generally the case in our parishes. The Irish landlord will do nothing. He exacts his rents, but to improve or repair is no part of his system. More than this, if the tenant improves or repairs, his rent is at once raised, or he is ejected in favour of a higher bidder. What can *we* do? And if we remonstrate and take the part of the people, we are at once branded as disloyal."

I had nothing to reply to this, and we remained silent for some time.

"Mr. Wyville," at length said the Priest, "I am glad of this opportunity of speaking with you on another subject. You were at Ballybog a few days ago. May I take the liberty of asking what took you there?"

"Mere accident; I lost my way, and wished to make inquiries."

"But another person was there also, and on the same day. I presume this coincidence was not the effect of design?"

"Certainly not."

"I am satisfied," replied the Priest, "I

thought it could not be. I was afraid that your companion in the boat on that day might be also the person who attempted to intrude herself on the solitude of my friends. You have heard, doubtless, of the Donovans?"

"Very little; I merely know that there is such a family in the country."

"There is only a father and a daughter, and an old servant who has been long with them, I believe, and whose daughter acts as female attendant. Circumstances of no consequence to any but themselves have induced them to retire thither, and any attempts to invade their voluntary seclusion is disagreeable to them. They were consigned to my protection by a dear friend, and are supposed to be my relatives, and I accordingly am sometimes admitted. You will perfectly understand my meaning in mentioning thus much to you."

I bowed my assent, and we were for some time silent. A thought suddenly struck me.

"Then am I to understand from you, sir, that no one but yourself visits at that house?"

"I am not aware that they either see or wish to see any one else."

We had now reached the Castle point. The Priest landed, and wished me good night, and I watched his dark form in the moonlight as he slowly ascended the rocky pathway, till he disappeared. My curiosity was awakened. Archibald must be playing a deep game of deception. That he had effected an entrance there, and that his designs were none of the most honourable, I could easily believe. Florence, whose rare intelligence and somewhat unscrupulous daring, had dived into his secret, was manifestly uneasy about her brother and his designs, and the caution she displayed in her endeavours to thwart them, evinced how much she feared his knowledge of her interference.

A new feeling took possession of me. Was this poor, unsophisticated girl, probably her father's sole stay and comfort, to be sacrificed to the unhallowed licentiousness of one who was already engaged to another? Knowing what was going on, was I to stand by, an unconcerned spectator? Florence had more than once adjured my aid. Was I right in withholding it? These were perplexing questions, not to be solved in a moment. Do what I would I could not get rid of them, and after a restless night I determined to see Florence once more before I decided on anything.

"Well, Frank," said my uncle Rosse, as I laid down my manuscript, "if ever a silly fly suffered himself to be caught in a flimsy web, you are the one. Did you not see how that Irish girl was winding round you? Having got you into a scrape, she would do anything to shield you—she did not care one atom for herself—oh, no! She would tell falsehoods—encourage the young blockhead she meant to throw overboard—anything to show how devoted she was to you! Like the poor fly and the treacle, you will look and sip till you are fairly caught and done for. What business, sir, had you to intermeddle in the affairs of Ballybog? Surely that old priest had wit enough to look after that wild girl. Egad, Frank, she served you right. I should like to know more of her and her great dog."

"You will hear more of her, sir, by-and-by. But I think you are hard upon Florence. I never saw her play off any such tricks as you describe; she is a high-spirited, independent girl. I could trust my life with her."

"And your heart, also, of course. I fancy, Master Frank, that all this romance of yours is but a preparation to announce your engagement to, or perhaps marriage with this dark-eyed Milesian, and the end of it is to be that I am to act as a mediator, and break the matter to the Admiral?"

"I know, sir, you are all kindness, and would do anything to serve me. But we must not anticipate events. Give me a patient hearing, and do not expect to find *your* wisdom and experience in a young man of twenty-three."

"My dear boy, I never looked for anything of the kind, and if the truth must be told, in my younger days I could not have trusted myself in such a position as yours. There is, after all, something rather good about the girl, and she was right, I think, in wishing to prevent her brother making a fool and a scoundrel of himself."

CHAPTER XII.

"Patience and Sorrow strove who should express her goodliest." *Cymbeline.*

FATE or accident, or whatever else you may call it, often brings about what all our ingenuity could not effect,—a proof of which I am now about to relate. The weather was still fine and open, with occasional white frosts, and as I had now much leisure on my hands, and the fishing season was closed, I preferred spending it on the hills, to lounging away my time at Mount Patrick, which I was often invited to do.

One morning I crossed the Lough, and ordered the boys to meet me in the evening at Flynn's cottage, and with Larry and the dogs took to the mountains. We had a glorious walk and enough of game to keep up the excitement. Larry was in high spirits, and as we ate our luncheon on the brink of a small tarn, which, like the crater of a volcano, was immured high amid lofty and precipitous crags, he referred to the party at Doonore.

"Sure the gintleman at the Mount has looked very crooked at me ever since I spilled the praties. And it was I that was glad that you won the elegant cup at the archery meeting, master. Siz I to Dan McBride, siz I, 'Dan, it's a pity Miss Florence and our master did not buckle together for the prizes; I'd have backed them two agin the whole field;' siz he, 'So would I Larry.'"

"By-the-bye, Larry Lannigan," said I,

"how was it you could be so awkward as to upset the potatoes?"

"Awkward, is it? It was not awkward at all. Did not you see, master, that I did it on purpose?"

"On purpose? You dare not do that. A dish of scalding hot potatoes on Mr Fitzpatrick's lap! I wonder he did not kill you."

"I'm not so easily kilt, master. And sure yourself knows all about it."

Larry looked round slily, and resumed eating his dry crust, for it was Friday. A conviction at once came across me that the fellow knew more of my proceedings than I had chosen to reveal, and to ascertain this I gave him the rein.

"What is it I know all about?" said I, fixing my eyes upon him. Larry did not speak, but continued masticating his crust. "I ask you again, what is it I know?"

"It is not exactly what you know, master, but what I know as well as yourself. By dad, we boys know many a thing we seem not to know at all, at all, or else how should we be after doing the master a service?"

"A service? What service have you done me? Larry, don't be making a gommagh of yourself."

"Well, then, to be plain, master, I upset the praties because I saw you and the *gintleman* that went with you in the boat was like to be in a boderation, the two of you at once."

"And what can you know about the *gentleman* in the boat? You never saw him."

"No, sure, I could not see him, and I did not see *him*, but I saw a fine young lady, mighty sweet entirely to look at, with a broad blue ribbon in her bonnet, get out of the boat, and get into it again, not a hundred miles from Lynn's cottage."

At once I perceived that our secret was known, and to admit Larry into my confidence, and to disabuse his mind of the impression I perceived had got possession of it, became my only and best policy.

"You know, then, who the lady was?"

"By the powers of war, and why not? Wasn't she sitting with the master quite alone by herself in the ould ruins at Glenlara Bridge, and did not she prefer him to that unfortunate sky-bow, young Titus O'Toole, of the Thrinity College, Dublin, and is not she many a morning and evening standing on the wooden bridge among the bushes for nothing at all but to take the fine air as is good for her health; and—"

"No more, Larry," said I, surprised and annoyed; "I never wish you to take any further notice either of Miss Fitzpatrick or of me—you are altogether wrong. We are mere friends and neighbours, nothing more, and your watching and interference in any way can only do harm, and give rise to groundless suspicions."

"Interference!" ejaculated Larry, in surprise, and a little offended. "It is only natural that I should interfere for the master. I always thought you would be after putting your commedher on Miss Florence, and that you wished her to be after walking into Rathlynn as the young mistress. By gor! I fear the family think so, and it's hard to be coorting back."

"Larry, I never courted at all, and Miss Fitzpatrick would be as much surprised as myself to hear all this foolish talk. So no more of it."

"Is it serious you are, master?" said Larry, with an anxious look; "for if you are, there is a strong breeze blowing up, and it must be looked to in time."

"I am serious, never more so in my life," said I; and we rose to pursue our sport.

As the sun was now declining, I sent Larry home with the game-bag and dogs, and throwing my gun on my shoulder I marched away in the direction of Flynn's cottage. My thoughts rambled to the past. It was manifest that Larry had been, as he thought, a busy and able coadjutor in my supposed matrimonial projects, and on reviewing every little circumstance I could perceive his instrumentality in many things that surprised me at the time, and I could not but fear that he had in many ways also compromised me with Florence herself.

What he meant by "a strong breeze blowing up," I could not understand, for I had never given either Mr. or Mrs. Fitzpatrick, or any one else, reasonable cause to suppose that I was seeking a connection with their daughter. And yet I did not feel quite easy.

It is difficult for the most wary to steer clear of the shoals and quicksands of life, and I could only resolve to be cautious for the future.

Thus musing, I strode along, and, descending the mountain side, soon found myself in a direct line with the lake, whose distant waters were now faintly tinged with the last crimson tints of the autumnal sun. On my left was a vale cheerless and dreary, betraying no signs of human habitation, but having a road running through it in a southerly direction. Looking towards this point I thought I could discern a figure moving, and I fancied, too, that a faint sound, as of a person in distress, came to my ears, borne on the western breeze.

I stopped, gazed, and listened eagerly, till I felt convinced that something was occurring which demanded instant attention. I at once fired off one barrel of my gun, and, as if in answer, I perceived the figure below me waving a white handkerchief, doubtless to attract notice.

Hastily reloading my gun, for I did not know what might be enacting below, I hurried down, and approached a kind of low ruined shed that stood by the road side; and on the margin of a sluggish bog-stained stream, I there saw a female figure beckoning to me impatiently. and then disappear within the shed. I entered, and there, on a pile of heath and fern was stretched the figure of a man struggling violently under the influence of an epileptic attack.

"Oh, sir, what can—what shall I do?" questioned the weeping girl, wringing her hands. "We are far from home, and there is no one to help us, unless you will kindly do so."

"That I will with pleasure," said I, "if you will only tell me how."

"I cannot leave my father, and without further assistance we shall never get him home."

"Then I will either remain with him, while you go, or shall I go myself?"

"A thousand thanks—you will be there quicker than I can—if it is not too much trouble. If I am not taking too great a liberty, oh, kind sir, would you hasten there, and bring our servant and the car."

"I will go at once; but where is your home? Can you point out the road?"

"The pathway up yonder hill will lead you to—to Ballybog."

This was my first sad introduction to the inmates of Ballybog. In the hurry and bustle consequent on the old man's removal to his home I had little time for observation, my whole attention being absorbed in conveying him as easily as possible along the rough road that led to the house. Road, indeed, it could scarcely be called. It was a mere passage cut through thickets and underwood, and not easily discovered by any but the inmates themselves. Mr. Donovan, for so was the sick man named, was considerably better ere he reached the house, and he tendered his thanks in that rapid and abrupt way that discovered, as I fancied, some portion of eccentricity in his manners and character. He begged me to stay and accept some refreshment, but as this request was not backed by the daughter, who stood silently and abstractedly by his couch, I at once took my departure, after making on my part a request—which was, however, received in silence—that I might be permitted ere long to call and inquire how the invalid was progressing.

The following day I took the skiff and rowed at once up the Lough, unaccompanied, to inquire after Mr. Donovan. I took the same path once before attempted by Florence on her first visit to the spot, and after walking a few hundred yards found myself in a copse, above which, against the blue sky, was visible the smoke of a dwelling. As I approached nearer there was a violent barking, and before I had emerged from the woodland the old servant met me, holding up his hand, as if to bar my further progress.

"The young mistress desired me to say that master is well again, and they both wish to thank your honour kindly for what you did yesterday."

"Can't I see them? I have come up the Lough to inquire after them. Surely they will not refuse to see me?" I slipped a douceur into Thady's hand, which, without appearing to notice it at once, changed his tone into one of exceeding civility.

"They don't like to be seen," said he, in a low tone, "for raisons of their own, and I was ordered to stop your honour, as I've stopped many a one afore you. But we know you have a will of your own, so you have only to rush past me, and you will find them both sitting under the porch."

I accordingly went forward, and not seeming to heed old Thady's remonstrances, who was shouting at the top of his voice,—

"Millia murthers—weirasthree—come out of that, now—back this way, &c., &c."

As I approached the porch slowly I had time for observation. In an easy chair sat Mr. Donovan, his daughter standing beside him with her hand clasped in his. They seemed to be quietly contemplating the scene before them—the smooth lake, the silent mountains. He was a fine old man, tall and muscular, but his countenance was pale and haggard, and his locks of silvery white fell upon his shoulders. He appeared weak and languid, probably the effect of his recent attack.

His daughter, like a guardian angel, was bending over him. Her costume was simple and even coarse, scarcely better than that worn by the peasantry of the country. A short blue cloak partly covered her head, and fell down gracefully upon her shoulders, partially hiding an abundance of fine glossy hair, which was only confined by a simple fillet. She seemed the perfect model of the superior peasant girl of the mountains, and there was an indescribable grace about her youthful and as yet scarcely well-developed form. And yet beyond this there was nothing particularly striking at first sight.

The expression of her countenance was anxious and sorrowful, and all her regards seemed fixed upon her father. My old enemy, the large dog, was lying at her feet, and looked up into her face, as much as to ask whether he was again to banish the intruder.

"Down, Bruno, down," said she, advancing to greet me. "My dear father is much better, and joins me in many thanks for your kind assistance yesterday. You will excuse my inviting you to enter the house; indeed, we have no accommodation, and we see no company."

A deep blush overspread her countenance, and I could perceive that my presence was irksome to them.

"Pardon my intrusion," said I, with a look of the deepest sympathy. "I could not but feel interested in knowing how Mr. Donovan was, and you must allow that it was my duty to make the inquiry."

"Oh, certainly, and we are very much obliged."

"Then allow me to speak one word to him," said I, advancing.

The old man, seeing me approach, raised himself in his chair, and his manner exhibited signs of better days.

"I came to inquire after you, sir," said I, taking his proffered hand, "and I hope you have recovered your attack of yesterday?"

"I have—they are short and frequent. You see me, sir, where I ought not to be; I am a broken-hearted old man."

'Oh, no, dear father," hastily interrupted the daughter; "you know we are very happy here, and have nothing in all the world to break our hearts about. This gentleman is a stranger to us, so you must not say such things."

"Stranger or not, Mary, dear, he has eyes, and he can see. I tell you again, sir, I am broken-hearted and miserable, and not accustomed to such a life, and in such a place as this. She likes it, and she can sing and be merry, and talk of fine scenery and beautiful walks, and the sweet fresh air of these mountains, but I know nothing of it, and never can."

"Dear father, do not talk thus to this strange gentleman. You know the only step we could take was to retire here, and did not Father Roche say you ought to be more than satisfied?"

"Father Roche—he? Oh, yes, the Jesuit—they will say anything. He brought us here, did he not, Mary?"

I saw the poor gentleman's mind was bewildered and weakened, probably by his attacks. His daughter seemed pained and anxious, and I turned to go away. My gaze met hers. What eyes! but they were full of tears.

"I will not again intrude, Miss Donovan," said I, gently, "but would you allow me to speak one last word to you?" She walked with me across the lawn till we gained the path by which I had entered. "I merely wish you to promise that you will command my services in any way. I see, I know, the painful position in which you are placed. We are both strangers in the country. The consciousness that you have a friend to apply to in any emergency must be cheering. Permit me to be that person. I trust, as an Englishman, unconnected with these parts, you will never find your confidence misplaced in me."

"Thank you," replied she, coldly, "we have Father Roche as our friend. I trust we shall need no other."

As I gently rowed myself across the

Lough, I mused deeply on what I had witnessed. Who *was* this Mr. Donovan? Why did he seclude himself, and so unwillingly, too, at Ballybog? How had Archibald Fitzpatrick contrived to gain a footing there; or was Florence mistaken? &c., &c.

CHAPTER XIII.

> Rejoice, ye scaly tribes, and leaping, dance
> Above the waves, in sign of liberty
> Restored—the cruel tyrant is no more.
>
> *Somerville.*

A FORTNIGHT had now elapsed. I had seen nothing and heard nothing of the family at Ballybog, and they seldom occupied my thoughts. Notwithstanding a kind of gentlemanly air about Mr. Donovan, I half suspected they were of low rank, for often had I seen an Irish beggar with the manners of a prince. "For you see, master," as Larry once said to me, "in our counthry all things are upside down — the raal born gintlemen are in rags, and the low born 'houts' (mean fellows) ride to hounds and drink the claret." Mary Donovan, too! what was she but a mere peasant girl, or little better? She might be graceful, and her step that of a queen, but so were many of the lowest rank who wore neither shoes nor stockings. But then Mary Donovan did not speak the brogue, but pure English. That was a puzzle, altogether an enigma; but surely scarcely worth unravelling, at least by me.

The weather, though tranquil, had now become colder, and Archibald proposed to me one morning to take a boat and venture out into the bay, perchance we might meet with wild fowl, or even shoot a seal. These amphibious animals are most destructive to the salmon, and haunting the mouths of estuaries intercept the fish as they run up into the fresh water, and being thorough epicures will only feast on the shoulders, leaving the remainder to be devoured by less fastidious creatures. Sometimes a great quantity of valuable oil is extracted from certain parts, and the skin is well known for the various uses to which it is applied. There is no sport more exciting than seal-shooting, and none more encouraged by the owners of salmon fisheries. Larry and the boys accompanied us, and we took our guns and rifles, with a handspike and a harpoon attached to a long rope.

As we left the river the water was smooth as glass, and the sun promised at least his autumnal warmth. As I never had shot a seal, Larry proposed that we should run directly for a sand-bank about two miles from the shore, and taking our station off the northern side of it till the tide left it nearly bare, we should suffer the boat to ground, while we, quietly slipping out, should so shelter behind it that the wary animals would not see us. As the bank rose towards the centre, being there hard and rocky, this was easy to accomplish, and there we stood for a considerable time up to our knees in water under the shelter of the boat, waiting till the tide was at ebb.

In about an hour Larry proclaimed this to be the case, and crawling on his hands and knees up the side of the bank he gave one quick look over it, and returning, said, there were seven seals basking just at the edge of the water, and he was sure they had not been disturbed. Without one moment's delay, the wind now blowing softly towards us, we crawled forward, and on gaining the ridge a most curious sight presented itself. Seventy or eighty yards from us seven monsters were reposing on the sand, and one great black-and-white fellow appeared to me to be almost the size of a calf. No sooner were our heads above the ridge than a mighty scuffle took place—the alarm was given, and all the creatures, rolling, shuffling, and paddling, made for the water. I took a rapid aim at the black-and-white gentleman, and just as he was about to disappear in the water, my ball took effect in or near his head. He rolled over, and Larry, eager for the fray, and armed with the handspike, ran towards him and endeavoured to interrupt his further attempts to gain the water.

Stunned for the moment, the beast lay motionless, and to make things sure Larry aimed a deadly blow at his head, but in his agony, turning half round, the creature dealt the poor fellow such a blow with his tail that he was thrown back into the water, and Larry, handspike and all, were soon invisible altogether.

Great was our consternation. There the

great creature lay in its last agonies, vainly striving to roll into the water, while his companions ever and anon popped up their heads at a respectful distance, gazing with their large soft eyes, as if inquiring what had become of their companion.

But what had become of Larry? Like the seals he, too, at length emerged, for having fallen backwards into a deep hole, scooped out by some eddy, he did not at once right himself so as to ascend to the surface. No sooner, however, was he on land, and had given himself one shake, than he aimed a deadly blow at his antagonist.

"You double-distilled ould sthrap—bad cess to you," exclaimed he, repeating the blow, "sure was it not a favour I was doing you to put you out of your misery, you poor crawling 'ownshuck,' and you to sarve me that same."

"Be aisy, Larry," said Mick Daly, "sure

it was a message he sent you with to the other sales in the water — maybe it was 'his will' he was after troubling you with."

"It's right you are, Mick, entirely," said Larry, "and as you want to be informed about it, I may as well tell you that I and the other sales opened the will, and by goora he had left you a legacy, Mick Daly, and the executors sent their compliments, and desired you'd go down below to receave it."

All this while poor Larry was dripping wet, but like a true Irishman he must have his rejoinder, be his condition what it might. As we stood there, "taking saye," as the ancient deer-stalkers used to express it, of the huge beast I had killed—that is to say, cutting it up and preserving the parts from which the oil is obtained—the other seals at a respectful distance every now and then ascended to the surface, and seemed to be contemplating the fate of their companion.

Many a rifle ball whizzed close to them, but in vain, as their heads were again under water before the missile struck the very spot where they appeared. Archibald made one effective shot, so he said, but as the animal did not re-appear, and no one had observed it, little account was taken of the assertion. It was plain that he did not like my success unless counterbalanced by his own.

Ws spent the remainder of the day pursuing the wild fowl, which in every variety and in great numbers frequented the sandbanks at low tide, but as the weather was yet fine and open we had no great success. While Archibald and I were shooting, the boys and Larry were fishing, and had soon secured a large number of various sorts of fish, so that on the whole, when we turned our boat's head homewards, we might congratulate ourselves on "a good day."

Nothing, indeed, is more delightful and exciting than this species of sport, and I have often been surprised how men will prefer a barren day on the mountains or the lake, to certain amusement on the broad waters of the bay. Those persons who visit a country like this for the mere chance of what a few days or a week may produce, know indeed nothing of its capabilities for the sportsman. You may angle in the finest river or Lough in the island for a week and more, and you may go away, as many others do, and condemn them altogether as mere humbugs, high in character but low in performance. But you are wrong. A day, a week, bursts upon you of splendid sport; you scarcely know how to account for it, and then again all is dull and flat, and day after day you seem to hope against hope. No one really knows the capabilities of a lake or river but those *who live near them*, and often do I pity those poor tourists who travel from London to the far west with bundles of rods, and rolls of tackle, and volumes of flies, expecting to tell, when they return from their ten days' trip, of salmon hooked, played, and gaffed, and panniers filled with trout, brown, white, and weighty.

It is all a mistake, gentlemen. Leave your tackle at home, and if the weather is propitious and the water in good order, accompany some knowing angler of the neighbourhood, who, nine times out of ten, will furnish you with what is really requisite, quite as well or better than Kelly, or Daly, or even Farlow himself. And if, after all, you are disappointed, and exhibit at the close of the day nothing but a shabby assortment of small fry and gobbahauns, don't abuse the stream—rather say you believe *they* are there, but they are out of humour and won't rise. For a month together have I sometimes toiled and laboured, and no good came of it, and then a glorious day, worth a year's disappointment.

As the river is not suitable for boats more than half a mile above its junction with the sea, we left ours near the bridge which connects the districts on the right and left banks, and Archibald and I walked on together, directions being given to Larry to preserve the seal's skin, which I intended as a future appendage to the great hall at Penrhôs. Half way up the river is a weir over which it is possible for an active person to pass, and here Archibald stopped suddenly, and wished me a good evening.

"I thought you would finish the day with me," said I, surprised.

"I have business up the mountain," said he hastily, as if to end the subject, and was moving off, when I called him back.

"If you are going up the Lough, my boat is at this end, and much at your service."

"Thank you, but I am not going in that direction."

He strode off, and I stood for a moment watching him as he made his somewhat hazardous progress over the weir.

"I think I know your destination, young man," said I to myself; "and if your object is the seduction of that fair mountain maid I will thwart you if I can."

But how? That was the question. How *could* I interfere? In what way? For the house at Ballybog was to me an interdicted spot. Should I follow Archibald, and, by watching his proceedings, confirm or otherwise my suspicions? No—there was a sort of treachery in that: whatever I did should at least be done properly. I had no permission, no right to interfere with the Donovans. However, as Archibald had said he was not going in that direction, there was no harm in my rowing up the Lough; perchance I might obtain a sight of Mary Donovan myself. If I could but see her, I might elicit some information from her, and put her on her guard.

I hastened forward, and was soon rowing quietly under the western shore, where the deep shadow of the rocks and trees served in some measure to conceal my motions. And yet, as I went along, my reflections were none of the pleasantest. I still felt as if I was prying into affairs in which I had neither business nor authority to intermeddle. But then came the fact that Archibald had declared he was not pursuing the route I was taking, and therefore I could be in no error if I believed him to have spoken the truth; and, moreover, what certainty had I that his visits at Ballybog were not altogether a fable? I had only the assertion of Florence to the fact, and might she not be mistaken?

Thus musing, I rowed quietly, and, I fear, somewhat stealthily, up the Lough, till I neared Flynn's cottage, and running my boat into a deep cove formed by a fissure in the rocks, I fastened it securely, and bounded up the slope into the thick copse above, making my way in the direction of Ballybog.

There was a lofty eminence, thickly wooded and precipitous, which divided the cottage from the house of the Donovans. I was now on the summit of this, and pausing to take breath, I looked around with interest at the lovely view before me. It was a vast panorama of lake, wood, and mountain. As I stood, the sound of voices below me arrested my attention. Was it fancy? All was again silent, till at length I saw two figures pacing a long ledge of rock stretching far to the right, and immediately bordering the lake. In a moment I perceived that these persons were no other than Archibald Fitzpatrick and Mary Donovan!

It was all true then—the despicable plot was going on, and the victim was readily falling into the snare.

By some sudden impulse I descended from my elevation, and—how I know not—succeeded in placing myself in a position where I could see, and even hear somewhat of their proceedings. Well did I know how unscrupulous Archibald was, and the actual danger of this young creature in trusting herself in his power. Without any wish to pry into the conversation, but determined to shield her from any violence, I quietly retained my position.

As they paced the rocky platform, I could not refrain my admiration. With the mantilla as usual partly covering her head, and flowing in ample folds down her back, she moved along with easy and matchless grace. Her step was slow, yet firm, and the homeliness of her costume rather set off than diminished the perfect elegance of her figure.

By the few words that met my ear, for he spoke in a low tone, I conjectured that he was endeavouring to laugh away and calm her fears, for several times she stopped suddenly, and her eye sought a kind of narrow path that wound up the cliff beyond. On one occasion he attempted to wind his arm round her waist, but she indignantly repulsed him, and seemed in earnest remonstrance and entreaty. At length they neared the spot where I stood, and I could distinctly overhear what they said.

"I think you were very wrong, Mr. Fitzpatrick, to follow me here, and then to take advantage of my situation thus to annoy me. I cannot, and, indeed, I will not hear you. Nothing on earth could persuade me to leave my father."

"Indeed, dearest girl," said he, again vainly attempting to steal his arm round her waist, "you wrong me—I would not annoy you for the world—but do not forget that I have your secret, and that I have hitherto showed every wish to act generously towards you."

"Alas, alas! what can I do?" said the poor girl, in a paroxysm of distress; "surely you would not betray us and at once cause our ruin, and the certain death of my poor father? But," continued she, looking up, and gazing suspiciously upon him, "what is it you know about us? Perhaps, after all, you are only deceiving me to gain some purpose of your own. Tell me, then, what is it that you know about us, and who could reveal our affairs to you?"

"My dear girl, be assured of this, I do know all about you," said the lying scoundrel, for I could tell, by the very tone of his voice, that he was uttering a lie; "it is of no use, therefore, your acting this part any longer. If you will accede to my proposal I will be as silent as the grave, and you shall have in me a powerful friend and a legal protector as long as you live."

"Your proposal?—what proposal?" said Mary, stepping back, pride and injured modesty flushing her face with crimson.

"Nay, if you are so very coy and so very particular," answered Archibald, significantly looking round him, "just remember where you are—there is not one human being here to render you assistance—and all your cries would avail nothing. You are completely and altogether in my power, and I advise you not to make me an enemy when I am anxious to be a friend."

Alarmed for the poor girl, I looked anxiously to the spot where they stood. Archibald was near the edge of the rock, with his back to the water; Mary was half turned away from him, clasping her hands as if in despair.

"Oh! do not take advantage of my folly in coming so far from home unattended, Mr. Fitzpatrick!" said she, in an agony of fear; "allow me to return, and I will forgive all that has passed. It is wicked thus to take advantage of a poor girl like me, who has no one to help or befriend her. If you are a man, you will scorn such mean treachery towards a defenceless female. O let me return home, and I shall ever think of you with kindness!"

"Nonsense!" said he, "absolute folly to talk thus. I will be plain with you—I mean no ill. My intentions are honourable. But it has cost me days of trouble and anxiety to meet you alone, and do you think, now, that I am to be foiled? No, no, my pretty colleen dhas, here you are, and here you shall be till we understand one another better, you may take my word for it. Again I say my intentions are honourable, and I can really see no cause why you should be so offended with attentions which, I have reason to think, few women would not be pleased with. But this is all nonsense—you have been shy and reserved long enough to save appearances—so now let us quietly walk homewards like good friends, and talk the matter over."

I saw him attempt to take her hand, and,

eager to shield her from further insult, I was rapidly descending the rock when I heard a sudden plunge in the water, then a scream, and then the sound of rapidly retreating footsteps. I paused for a moment, and all was still.

CHAPTER XIV.

"If I do vow a friendship, I'll perform it."
Othello.

HASTE often foils itself. My anxiety to reach the scene of action was intense, and careless of everything but my object, I slid down through a thick bush of briars, with the intention of gaining the rocky platform below me. But the hazard of not first reconnoitring my position soon became painfully apparent—a deep fissure separated the ledge of rock from the higher ground on which I had stood, and into this I found mvself sliding rapidly down. My situation was perilous in the extreme, and it was only by holding firmly by the stem of a mountain ash that I arrested my progress, and after many violent efforts at length obtained a secure footing, with the dark abyss gaping below me.

It was some time, notwithstanding all my exertions, before I was safely landed on the rocky ledge. I looked around anxiously, but nothing was to be seen. Was it Mary Donovan or Archibald that had fallen into the water? I examined the spot, but there was no sign. In that particular place the water was very deep—but not a ripple was to be seen. Some splashing was visible on the rock, indicating that my surmise was just, some one had fallen in, but who? A most dreadful suspicion crept over my mind—Mary Donovan, in her eagerness to escape his violence, had thrown herself into the water, preferring death to dishonour.

And he, the scoundrel, what had become of him? Sneaked away, probably, hoping to conceal his crime and its consequences.

Often and often I paced the platform, and gazed into the deep, clear waters, perchance I might obtain a glimpse of the body of this poor girl—but no—I could see nothing—around was silence deep as death—not even a ripple of the lake murmured amongst the rocks—what was to be done? Of course it was my first duty to see the inmates of Ballybog, and acquaint them with the fearful fact of which I was so unhappily cognizant. I therefore bent my steps that way, following a kind of sheep track that seemed to wind up the side of the eminence that intervened between Ballybog and the place where I now was.

It led me into a deep and narrow glen, divided on the left from the Lough by a low barrier of rock, and on the right hedged in by a range of lofty crags, half covered with clinging ivy, and exhibiting from many a crevice graceful masses of holly, mountain ash, and sombre yew.

Making my way up this lovely gorge, I at length came to a spot which was beautiful in the extreme. Here the broad expanse of the Lake burst upon the sight, and north and south seemed to wind in among the mountains, till lost in the far distance. Here, too, as if nature had provided accommodation for the admiring wayfarer, a commodious seat was formed naturally in the rock. Near this platform, and close to the seat, three young oaks cast a sheltering shade, and a sweeter and more romantic seclusion on a bright summer's day could not be imagined.

Here, to my astonishment—to my delight—sat Mary Donovan—she whom my imagination had already consigned to a watery grave! What a relief was this! She sat on the rock, as if resting from some violent fatigue. Her face was deadly pale—she trembled as if under the influence of recent agitation; her bonnet was on the ground at her feet, and her luxuriant tresses, having escaped the fillet that bound them, wantoned in beautiful disorder over her shoulders.

"Thank God, Miss Donovan," said I, approaching her, "that you are here. I feared that villain had destroyed you."

She did not answer, but motioned me to pass on.

"No," replied I, to her silent appeal, "I will not leave you now—I will see you safe to your home."

"Pray go forward, Mr. Wyville, and leave me here. I assure you I need no assistance. In a few minutes I shall be with my father."

She rose and began to ascend the rocky

path up the dingle. I was not to be thus repulsed, particularly under circumstances of so extraordinary a nature.

"Where is your late companion, Miss Donovan?" said I, walking by her side, though with some difficulty, owing to the narrowness of the path; "I thought I heard a plunge in the water."

"It was Mr. Archibald Fitzpatrick," replied she with a shudder.

"And where is he now?" I inquired, although almost afraid of what might be the answer.

"He regained the shore. There he is," continued she, pointing down the lake.

I looked, and perceived a boat rounding the promontory. I knew the boat at once, and a heavy weight passed from my mind. All was as it should be—the miscreant had met with a well-merited and mortifying repulse, and, so far, no real harm was done.

But what of the future? I knew Archibald too well not to be aware of the danger which still environed Miss Donovan.

"Knowing, as I do, all the facts of the case," said I to her, soothingly, "may I ask what course you will pursue?"

"I cannot tell," replied she, in a low voice, "we are, I fear, too much in his power to resent his conduct as we ought; or rather," continued she, as if checking herself, "we are too powerless and helpless to obtain any reparation, or even, I fear, to defend ourselves."

The tears forced their way through her beautiful eyelashes, and trembled on her fair cheek.

"Oh, Mr. Wyville!" said she, suddenly stopping, and turning to me, "do not involve yourself in our affairs—you do not know the danger, but I foresee it all. I would not that your generous interference should bring trouble upon yourself. To you as well as to us, this is a strange country and a strange people. We have no friends here—either you or ourselves."

"The more cause that we should be friends to each other," replied I, quickly. "Miss Donovan, you may decline my offers of service, but I will watch over you, and, if need be, will defend you and yours, even against your will. I were unworthy of my name and nation, did I suffer this species of oppression to proceed under my very gaze. If you will give me your confidence, you shall find in me a steady friend and adviser. If you repulse me, I will, nevertheless, watch you, though at a distance, and, as far as I can, will shield you from such unmanly and dangerous annoyance."

We had now gained the summit of the gorge, and had paused an instant to regain our breath. She looked for one moment earnestly and anxiously in my face. I could perceive that she was favourably affected by what I had said. For a short time, with her eyes on the ground, she seemed buried in her own reflections—then looking up more cheerfully, she gave me her hand, and said,—

"I do not mistrust *you*, Mr. Wyville—I have the fullest confidence in your kindness and generosity, and I am sure my poor dear father will accept your offers of service. It is, of course, with him, not with me, that you must concert measures to put a stop to this odious persecution; and yet," continued she, as if in great perplexity, "and yet—what can—what will my father say or do?—alas! he is incapable of defending either himself or me!—No, no, sir—accept our gratitude for your kindness, but I do not see how you can aid us."

"But I do, Miss Donovan. Your situation here is too peculiar to bind you down to common rules of action—you must banish all this reserve, and rely with confidence on my honour."

"I cannot doubt your honour, but——"

"No buts—the case is plain—you confess yourself weak and defenceless—you are far from friends, from assistance. I freely offer you—or if you will rather have it so, your father, my friendship and my aid. Is it prudent to reject my offer?"

We walked on in silence till the chimneys of Ballybog were seen peeping from the grove in which the house was buried.

"I will now say farewell," said she, "with many thanks for your kindness, and may I request, Mr. Wyville, that you will not mention to any one the events of this day. Adieu!"

"But you have not answered my proposal," said I, hurrying after her.

With a rapid step she had already gained the copse, and was out of sight in a moment.

Strange girl! thought I, as stopping, I gazed upon the spot where she had disappeared. That independent spirit will be thy ruin—thy very modesty will make thee the easier mark—like Beatrice—

"Thy spirits are as coy and wild as haggards of the rock;"

but in spite of thyself, I will guard and protect thee, poor, defenceless girl!

Thus resolved, I quietly returned home, meditating as I went on all these things.

I was never accounted romantic. I do not think that my nature is peculiarly excitable, nevertheless, the fortunes of the mysterious inmates of Ballybog did strangely interest me. I could not tell why, and yet my feelings were drawn towards them with a strong and strange sympathy. I no longer needed the injunctions of Florence Fitzpatrick to urge me on; my own heart prompted to me the course I should pursue, and this was, to disobey Florence in one particular at least, and to make myself better acquainted with the Donovans and their fortunes. 'Tis true I had met with little or no encouragement from the daughter, but with the father I might be more successful. That there were unpleasant, perhaps hazardous passages in his history, I felt assured—but what they were, and how they were to be unravelled, I could not tell. I must trust to chance to give me the power to serve them.

My position with the Fitzpatricks was now an awkward one. That they fancied I had been seriously attentive to Florence was evident enough. How I was to act with regard to Archibald himself was a most perplexing question, after all I had known and seen. I felt that without any fault on my side, there were "breakers ahead." How was I best to meet them? I thought of Father Roche, and after much consideration, determined to call upon him, and be guided by my own observations as to how far I could trust him, either for advice or assistance.

That was a wild valley in which the priest lived. It had once been thickly peopled, as the numerous remains of mud cabins and patches of gardens too plainly proved. But famine, and disease, and emigration had done their work, and those lands once bustling with life were now a bare and desert wilderness. But the Chapel was still there, and the cross that surmounted its lowly gable, and the old burial ground, and the priest's house, that stood unsheltered on the barren mountain side. It was a picture of desolation not uncommon in Ireland, and arising from a social system that could have no other result, but which now, we may hope, is rapidly disappearing.

And how can a man of the world—a man of enlightened views like this priest—endure to pass his days in such a solitude? Such were my thoughts as I reached the door, which was opened by the priest himself. He received me courteously, and on entering his little parlour I found a picture of comfort within that little accorded with the desolate scene without. Cleanliness, a bright fire, and many indications of creature comforts greeted my admittance;—there was a small but good collection of books, many of them foreign, and a housekeeper brought in refreshments on a tray, who, by her staid, quiet manner, and the neatness of her costume, and freedom from the brogue, convinced me that she had no claim to Celtic origin. Father Roche would enter upon no conversation till I had done justice to the fare set before me, and drunk a glass or two of such sherry as our English wine-merchants can seldom furnish. He said he had it directly from Spain, in which country he had friends.

There was something so kind and so trustworthy in the manner of the priest—so little of sectarian insolence and native vulgarity—that I felt he was very superior to his order, as developed in Ireland, and I accordingly resolved to trust him without reserve, and, in a few words, detailed all I knew and had observed relative to the position of the family at Ballybog. He heard me calmly to the end, and then, leaning his head upon his hand, seemed to be deeply weighing matters in his own mind.

"All this is very sad and very wrong, Mr. Wyville," said he, at length, "and how to act is to me peculiarly perplexing. The Fitzpatricks are not only Protestants, but stand forward on all occasions as the determined opponents of the Catholic Church. For me to interfere in these matters would raise a great commotion: I shall be told to confine myself to my own flock, and to mind my own business—I shall be accused of Jesuitically worming myself into family secrets that do not concern me; in fact, I must keep clear of the whole thing, further than advising my friends at Ballybog to be on their guard, and, if need be, to apply to the civil power for protection. More than this I cannot do."

"But are not those friends placed there under your special protection?"

"As Protestants they are not under my special protection. Mr. Donovan married a distant relation of mine, and a kind of friendly feeling has ever been kept up. He was in difficulty and in danger, and applied to me for advice. This brought him to Ballybog. I seldom see them—indeed, we have few common sympathies. But this poor girl, I feel much for her. A more devoted daughter to a somewhat morose and moon-stricken father cannot be conceived. He is bound down by a series of the most impracticable delusions. I speak confidentially, Mr. Wyville. What they are you will yourself doubtless learn. They have, however, proved his ruin, and involved him in those difficulties which he has come here to escape. Probably some accident has acquainted young Mr. Fitzpatrick with Donovan's position, and he is taking advantage of this knowledge so to terrify the unhappy girl that her very devotion to her father will prove the best aid to his wicked designs."

"But we must foil them, sir—I will never

allow him to succeed in such an iniquitous attempt. He is engaged to another. I feel a more than common interest in these people, and, at all risks, will stand their friend."

"You are young and ardent, Mr. Wyville, and your feelings and intentions do you credit. But reflect a moment. Are you prepared for a feud with a family who are backed in the country by a large following? The Fitzpatricks are violent people. You will, I assure you, be worsted in the contest. If you would be useful to our poor friends, it must be quietly and unostentatiously. Do not let young Fitzpatrick know that you are aware of his proceedings; but as to his sister," continued the priest, smiling, "I must leave you to your own imaginings. She is a fine young woman, and of a decided character; but how far any female is to be trusted in affairs of this sort you know probably better than I."

"There can be no objection to my formally making the acquaintance of the Donovans?"

"None in the world, that I know of. You, like them, are unconnected with the country, and I see no reason why you should not be friends. Indeed it is in this way only that you can assist them, should need be; and," continued the priest, looking me steadily in the face for a moment, "I know you will do no one act inconsistent with your character as an Englishman and a gentleman. Of this I feel assured."

I bowed, and the conversation now turned on indifferent matters. On the following day, I promised to accompany Father Roche to Ballybog, where I was to be introduced as his friend.

END OF VOL. I.

CPSIA information can be obtained
at www.ICGtesting.com
Printed in the USA
LVHW101345160422
716387LV00003B/184

9 783752 594591